Also by Donna Huston Murray

The Lauren Beck Crime Novels:

WHAT DOESN'T KILL YOU
Honorable Mention, The 23rd Annual Writer's Digest
Self-Published Book Awards

GUILT TRIP

The Ginger Barnes Main Line Mysteries:

THE MAIN LINE IS MURDER

FINAL ARRANGEMENTS

SCHOOL OF HARD KNOCKS

NO BONES ABOUT IT

A SCORE TO SETTLE

FAREWELL PERFORMANCE

LIE LIKE A RUG

And Traditional Mystery:

DYING FOR A VACATION

FOR BETTER OR WORSE

A Ginger Barnes Main Line Mystery #8

By Donna Huston Murray

Copyright © 2018 Donna Huston Murray
ISBN #978-0-9861472-0-3

Please feel free to contact the author via her website:
donnahustonmurray.com

Chapter 1

THE MORNING the deceased came into my life I woke up with a start, the way I had when I was a kid. Lifting my head from the pillow, I squinted at pale June daylight leaking through the gap in the bedroom drapes. No doubt about it; I felt different.

Eager.

Ambitious.

Nearly as happy as my former self: Ginger Struve Barnes, mother of two, DIY enthusiast, and wife of Robert Ripley Barnes, the esteemed, green-eyed, and wickedly funny head of Bryn Derwyn Academy.

During the three years since my husband's fatal accident on an icy stretch of I-95, the words "eager," "ambitious," and "happy" seldom described my mood. Yet lately I have felt physically lighter—never mind that the bathroom scale disagreed. I've also caught myself saying "Yes" more often than "No," especially to invitations.

I've rejoined the world! I told Rip telepathically. *How about that?*

Go for it, babe, he replied, just as I knew he would.

To break the silence, at times I said these things out loud. Never in public though, so what was the harm?

I also talked to my dog. Soon after the accident, I discovered the muddy derelict digging for table scraps in the neighbor's compost pile. He wasn't wearing a collar, so I dutifully posted signs and even advertised for his owner. No one called; I had myself a new pet.

Fideaux responded as any physically and emotionally starved animal would, but surprise, surprise. I did, too. I slept better touching the rangy mutt's curly gray fur. On my worst nights he licked away my tears. If I sighed, he sighed. Whenever I began to feel sorry for myself, he rested his chin on my foot and worried about me.

"Up and at 'em," I woke him with a nudge on that lovely morning. "We have things to do, people to see."

He lumbered off the bed and stretched before trotting toward the kitchen door.

I poured kibble and freshened Fideaux's water before hustling back to get dressed. Since I'd be alone putting down peel-and-stick tiles at my newlywed daughter's house, I chose my oldest green t-shirt, the one that said "Alaska or Bust." And jeans, always jeans. I splashed my face, fluffed my short reddish hair.

"Ride in the car," I informed the dog the instant we finished breakfast.

The newlyweds had purchased a promising fixer-upper in a cozy, treed settlement nine miles by turnpike from where I live. Rush-hour traffic clogged the exit, but when I broke free of the entrance to an industrial park, it was only another three minutes to my destination, a yellow, three-story Victorian close to Chelsea's teaching job and Bobby's train commute.

The house sat shoulder to shoulder with its neighbors but possessed a lengthy backyard. Due to some missing fence Fideaux needed to be leashed and supervised back there, a time-consuming chore I preferred to get out of the way before starting the kitchen floor. Unfortunately, the morning's gray-white sky had lowered during my commute, and the air felt thick with drizzle.

While Fideaux dithered and sniffed, sniffed and dithered, I planned how to go about laying the floor tiles. Tidy up first, then make sure the old Formica was clean and sound. Snap a line to get a square start—for sure the old walls would be off; they always were...

Whump.

I jumped. Fideaux growled. Then we both gravitated toward the sound.

Someone had thrown a loaded garbage bag from the third floor of the somber gray Victorian to the left. It landed beyond a shallow cement patio and split, spewing clothes and bricks in a messy heap.

Bricks? I hoped no child had taken such a chance.

I raised up on tiptoes for a better look over the shrubbery-lined fence.

Yes, bricks.

"Hey!" I shouted up to the wide-open window.

No response. Just a gaping black rectangle, no screen, nothing and nobody visible beyond the opening.

Maybe the woman of the house had been cleaning out a closet, tossing her kids' outgrown clothes, or purging her own unwanted dreck. Faced with carrying a loaded bag downstairs for disposal, I might have tried the three-story drop, too. Once anyway. If nobody was around.

And nobody was supposed to be around. The house in question was the last on the block, Chelsea and Bobby were both at work, and I was here merely by chance.

But bricks?

That was just plain creepy.

Chapter 2

CHELSEA BARNES *ALCOTT,* she still wasn't used to her new name, tuned out her boss's voice and scanned the other faculty members dotting the auditorium. Sprawled across two seats like a teenager, the soccer coach appeared to be asleep. The Spanish teacher was filing her nails; and up front a new hire paid rapt attention, unaware of the rest of her colleagues zoning out behind her. Unless the information strayed too far from her own subject, which happened to be music, last year Chelsea had been that woman.

A sudden silence riveted the room. Hands on his hips, the head of school glared at his audience.

"Back in fifteen, people," he ordered.

So he'd noticed, Chelsea realized. Good for him.

She got moving, quick before he changed his mind. But where to go? What to do? She was torn between running for the coffee table and stepping outside to phone her mother. All the text message said was, "Please call."

Sighing with resignation, Chelsea headed for the door. After the morning's drizzle, the brightness of the quad came as a shock.

"Yes, Mom. Thanks, Mom. Go for it," she responded to Gin's detailed question. The new flooring *should* extend into the pantry at the top of the basement stairs. That would require more tile and a thick piece of plywood to bring the extra area up to level, but no problem. If Home Depot had had a bridal registry back when her parents married, Ginger Struve Barnes would have been on it.

A glance at her watch. Enough time for coffee, unless…

"By the way, who lives on your left facing the street?" Gin inquired.

"Mrs. Zumstein," Chelsea answered cautiously. "She's about a hundred and two. Why do you ask?"

"Just curious. You know me."

"You're not going to adopt my whole neighborhood, are you?" She loved her mother; but Mrs. Zumstein would be a mere cheese straw to Gin, and a skimpy one at that. Before the last tile was in place, Bryn Derwyn Academy's Hostess Emeritas would make a meal of the entire neighborhood, and Chelsea and Bobby would end up feeling like newlyweds on reality TV.

"Of course not!" Gin proclaimed.

Other faculty members who had opted for fresh air were easing their way back into the building, so Chelsea ended the call.

Yet her heebie-jeebies lingered, and she thought she knew why. In her haste to prevent Ms. Fix-it from adding Mrs. Zumstein to her collection of eccentric friends, she'd opened her mouth and put the idea in her mother's head.

"Pink elephants," she muttered as she bypassed the coffee urn. "I'll never learn."

***

GRATEFUL FOR Chelsea's go-ahead, I bought a four by eight foot piece of five-eighths inch plywood, dragged it into the backyard, and settled it onto two overturned trash cans. By then sunshine had dried the grass, so I felt fairly confident I wouldn't electrocute myself using an electric saw.

Coming from Mrs. Zumstein's direction, the explosions—crack, pop...*pop*—occurred just after my first cut.

I yelped. Then I carefully lowered the circular saw to the ground before I dropped it. A smell that could well have been gunpowder wafted over the fence.

What now? Bolt inside to call 9-1-1? The three pops had been followed by nothing. No thumps or wild shrieking, no rapid footsteps. Other than the noise and the smell, nothing seemed out of the ordinary. This was the suburbs, after all, not Philadelphia. You can live your whole life here without ever hearing a gun go off.

I tiptoed over to the fence and crouched beneath the shrubbery.

After listening to silence for a few minutes, I gave up and returned to work.

Yet my mind refused to leave the troubling incident alone. Who was this Zumstein woman, and what was she up to? Bricks in a bag were one thing, but the pops were another. Not quite loud enough to rattle a windowpane, they were about what you'd expect from a handgun muffled by something.

The notion flashed me back to some experiences best forgotten, sudden deaths that skirted way too close to home. After several years of minding my own concerns, was I being sucked into yet another domestic intrigue?

Preposterous! I hadn't encountered a crime in ages and probably wasn't encountering one now. Like a bored kid on a rainy day, my mischievous brain was probably toying with me.

You're not going to adopt my whole neighborhood, are you?

Chelsea's admonition firmly in place, I finished the cuts I had measured, then wrestled the awkward piece of plywood back inside to the pantry.

When I tried to drop it in place, the right side stuck twelve inches off the floor.

"If at first you don't succeed," I muttered while I struggled to dislodge the heavy plywood.

Outside, the stink that either was or wasn't gunpowder seemed even stronger than before. Had I missed more shots while I was inside?

I left the four by eight on my makeshift sawhorses and sneaked back for another look over the fence.

Three wooden steps led directly from the kitchen to the cement patio the trash bag had so narrowly missed. Venturing as close as I dared, I noted the household objects littering the area below the door—an hibachi full of rusty water, a pot, a broken doll, a pair of moldy men's shoes, a crooked lamp, a watering can, and a tangle of coat hangers. No sign of the dropped trash bag or its disturbing contents.

Falling bricks were one thing, but the sound of gunfire was another.

"Hello!" I called over the fence. "Everybody all right in there?" If a large, scary villain appeared, at least I had a hammer and saw at my disposal and two sneakered feet ready to run.

I waited a moment then shouted louder. "Mrs. Zumstein! Are you alright?"

No answer. Perhaps the old lady had been doing something that made sense only to her and preferred to be left alone. Or, like the squeaks and creaks of any house, maybe it took time to get used to the normal sounds of a neighborhood.

I listened for a few more minutes; but when nothing stirred, I returned to my project.

Two more tries and I managed to make the plywood fit. A gap near the corner of the cellar steps had to be filled with a scrap of wood and some caulk, a miscalculation I might not have made had my focus been better; but when the tile was in place, the mistake wouldn't show.

An hour later the pantry area was ready to go. I opened a Diet Coke and, with my back to the refrigerator, slid my sweaty, dirty self to the floor. I had just taken the first cold sip when the trill of my cell phone made me jump.

"You're still coming, aren't you?" barked my best friend, Didi.

"To what?" I asked, wiping up spilled soda with my shirt tail.

"Dinner, of course. I knew you'd forget."

"Did not," I fibbed. "I just lost track of time. What time is it anyway?"

"Four-thirty. You're supposed to be here at five."

"Can Fideaux come, too?"

A pause. "If he must."

"On my way," I fibbed again. Then I hung up and ran for the stairs.

Chapter 3

THE MILLERS faced each other across the bedroom, anger coloring their complexions.

"You cannot fix up a widow who isn't ready to be fixed up," Will insisted. Topping his narrow face and long nose was a full complement of straight, sandy hair that flopped onto his designer glasses during heated moments. "Do you really want your best friend to hate you?"

"She won't."

"She might."

A semi-retired psychologist, Will wrote essays about television and modern-day man with the hope of compiling his observations into a book. Two afternoons a week he still saw patients, but thanks to the foresight of his late friend, Rip Barnes, the rest of his time was devoted to his third— and final—wife. He didn't mind admitting it; Dolores "Didi" Martin Miller fascinated him no end. Even their verbal sparring was fun.

Yet this time the unspoken five-minute limit had come and gone. He was right, dammit. Surely Didi would get that if he said it one more time.

"She'll hate you."

"Will not."

"Alright," he said, raking his hair back in place. "Let's look at this from the man's perspective. Why would a single guy, of a certain age—and you admit Gin needs somebody *of a certain age*—why would an available guy like that waste his time meeting a woman who still isn't over her husband?"

Didi huffed and whirled. Her warm blonde hair flared like a long skirt and fell against her flushed face.

"Are you listening to yourself? Do you hear what you're saying? Gin is adorable, I tell you. She's cute."

Will privately added *for her age.*

"She's smart."

Smart-mouthed, if you're being honest.

"She's handy with tools..."

"Now you're talking," he leaned toward his wife with puckered lips.

"William!" Didi scolded. "I'm making a point here."

"What? What point? That Gin is a hot date?"

The deflation was instantaneous. "No. I guess not. But she could be if she wanted to."

In honor of his wife's loyalty to her dear friend, which was admirable of course, Will gentled himself down. "That's just it, darling. Gin isn't ready."

"What if she's never ready?" Didi seemed almost teary as she glanced up at her husband's face.

"You look like a llama," she remarked.

"Do llamas have horns?" he asked with a crooked grin.

***

AT FIVE-FIFTEEN Didi opened the door of their large brick colonial and leaned forward to give her oldest friend a peck on the cheek. "Hello, Sweetie," she said, stepping back to let Gin enter, which was when she noticed what her guest was wearing.

"Whoa, there," she exclaimed, raising her professionally manicured hand like a stop sign. "Been robbing the rag bag again?"

"I was laying tile at Chelsea's, so I showered there." Raiding the closet of a daughter eight inches taller and two sizes thinner had been a challenge, but she'd found a stretchy, peach-colored sweater and a long, brown skirt that didn't quite cover her paint-stained sneakers.

"Please," Didi said with a wrinkled nose. "Don't move." She whirled off toward the stairs, leaving behind a pleasant herbal scent.

She returned bearing a pair of brown ballet-style slippers and a braided leather belt. "Put these on," she ordered.

The slippers fit. "Does this mean I have to point my toes?"

"The belt, too. We both know you have a waist."

"Waist not, want not," Gin quipped.

"You're going to be annoying tonight, aren't you?"

Gin's brow furrowed. "That depends. Who is this George person?"

"George Donald Elliot."

"No last name?"

Didi finally acknowledged the red flag waving in her face.

The woman she knew was far from shy. Whenever Rip's school held an Open House, she was the first person to stick out her hand and say, "Hi, I'm Ginger Barnes. Welcome to Bryn Derwyn Academy." That Gin presently exhibited signs of a sagging confidence worried Didi far more than any silly, nervous jokes.

She isn't ready, Will had insisted, and Didi finally saw it his way. If she were to lose him in a car crash on that treacherous I-95, she couldn't imagine ever wanting to date again.

Yet the principals were already here. She had to do something.

A distant winter evening came to mind. Both Will and Rip had been out, so the two girlfriends settled in front of the walk-in fireplace with pizza and margaritas to celebrate a local magazine article about Gin solving a murder. Didi remarked that Gin should hang out a shingle. "Problems Solved," the sign would read; "Problem Solver," the title on her business card. Additional margaritas prolonged the discussion until Gin had been forced to stay overnight.

"Just come in and meet him," Didi urged with no show of sympathy. After all, her dinner wasn't getting any younger.

The Miller's great room possessed a wall of windows overlooking an elaborate rock garden. Inside, the couple had bracketed a fireplace—large enough to roast an ox—with leather furniture, which in early June looked irrelevant and cold. Probably a second reason why the men stood by a bar in the far corner.

Didi gracefully waved a hand. "George, I'd like you to meet Ginger Barnes. Gin, this is George Donald Elliot." She swiftly added, "Will, please pour Gin's wine. I need George in the kitchen for a quick little minute."

George grasped Gin's outstretched fingers instead. His face ignited with such pleasant surprise that Didi couldn't help congratulating herself. Gin *was* cute, if you liked short, cinnamon hair styled slightly on the wild side and flashing dark eyes.

"Should I pick my favorite?" she addressed George, "or do you have one?"

His rapt expression dissolved. "Wha…? One what?"

"Name."

"Oh? Oh! Yes. My friends call me George."

"What do your enemies call you?"

"Ah, um, George."

Didi crooked a finger to remind him he was wanted in the kitchen.

He dispensed with whatever he had planned to say and excused himself.

Before the kitchen door completely shut, Didi noticed Gin holding her thumb and forefinger three inches apart while Will began to pour.

Outside, the resident apricot standard poodles, Fluffy and Muffy, yapped like maniacs at Fideaux in hopes of getting him to play. Didi pressed her forehead with a cool palm before addressing George.

"Do you have a problem?" she thought she asked pleasantly.

The man gawked at her, and the expression caused him to look like a bird of prey. "Have I done something wrong?" *already?*

"No, no, no," Didi answered as if she were perplexed. "Do you have some sort of problem you can ask Gin about? If you don't, I might be able to supply you with one…"

Even as she said it she wondered exactly what that could be. Gin's household repairs were best characterized as a hobby, and anyway there was some debate about how capable she was. No, George needed a life-shattering dilemma worthy of the Problems Solved business she and Gin had toyed around with that night.

She took a minute or two to explain.

"So. If by chance you have a nephew who shoplifts or a daughter with an unfaithful husband to be followed, something like that, Gin is the perfect person to handle either. The rest is up to you," she added weakly.

"I do have a selfish bastard for a son-in-law," George offered.

"Perfect," Didi exclaimed. "Let's get back in there."

Chapter 4

AFTER WE finished the gazpacho—store bought, if I knew Didi—she encouraged George to talk about himself.

"I consult back to my old insurance firm," he reported, "mostly handling the needs of two local universities, long-time customers of mine.

"I also sell if an opportunity presents itself," he elaborated, "but I don't go very far out of my way for that anymore."

"An opportunist," I observed.

"I suppose that's one way to put it." He blinked uncomfortably as he served himself a dollop of mashed potatoes. "Also, I've been divorced for a year."

Alarm flashed through me as swiftly as heat lightening.

"Do you play golf?" Will asked into the silence.

George answered no, then swiveled back toward me.

"Do you have family?" he inquired.

He didn't want more succotash, so I set the bowl aside. "A newlywed daughter and a son in college."

"Your son—what's his name?—where does he go?"

"Garret. University of Virginia."

"Oh! Good school," George exclaimed.

"Guess what Garry asked me to send down right after he arrived."

Didi guessed money.

"Food?" George offered, forking a bite of roast pork into his mouth.

"Nope. Golf clubs and a tuxedo."

"You're kidding."

"Afraid not. I told him I needed to see some grades before the clubs got the okay. But it seems they still dress-up down there, so I sprung for a used tux from a rental shop."

"I suppose he's home for summer?"

"Not yet. Somebody invited him to Cape Cod for a couple weeks."

"Making the most of his opportunities." George teased. Payback for my cheeky "opportunist" remark.

We all concentrated on our dinner for a bit. Then Didi stabbed the air with her index finger. "You know, Gin, George might have a problem for you to solve."

George swallowed hard.

"Something about your son-in-law?" Didi hinted.

"Yes. Yes! He's...he's just...not nice."

George's comfort zone was a tiny dot in his rearview mirror; but if he wanted me to become interested in him, this wasn't such a bad approach. I rested my chin on my fist and leaned in a little. "Does he abuse your daughter?"

"No. No! Nothing like that. At least I don't think so."

"Then what do you mean, not nice?"

"Not nice. He doesn't help Susan with the baby. Doesn't help her with anything that I can tell." He set down his utensils. Contemplated his empty dinner plate.

"Lots of people get marriage wrong the first couple of times." Didi's contribution, but she was on her second marriage, her husband on his third. "Right, dear?"

Her present spouse agreed, but that was clearly all he planned to say on the subject.

"You think that's all it is?" I pressed. "An unsuitable marriage?"

George fixed his hazel eyes on mine and admitted he didn't know.

"None of our business, is it, really?"

"No, I suppose not," he concurred.

I stared at my salad.

"I do have a client I can't find." A weak effort, but an effort nonetheless.

"Why do you need to reach him? Or her?" I asked just to be polite.

"I…ah…thought I'd…no reason. I just couldn't find him when I tried."

"Don't call me/I'll call you sort of thing?"

"Er…uh…yes, I guess so." Then suddenly the sun came out. "Susan's getting a part-time job. How would you like to babysit?"

"Me?" I glanced from George, to Didi, to Will, and back.

George nodded vigorously. "Three half days a week. They just moved here from Jacksonville and don't know many people. I said I'd ask around."

The prospect horrified me, but to be honest I had just enough income to keep me and mine housed and fed and dressed as long as I didn't become a world traveler or go in for collecting, well, anything. I had plenty of skills, but very few of them were marketable, and anyway I'd been spoiled by the freedom from employment Rip's job afforded me. However, putting Garry through college was proving to be a bigger drain on the budget than I'd anticipated. A *tuxedo,* for God's sake. What next? Lab fees and underwear?

"One kid? Two? Four? Eight?" I inquired.

"One boy about eighteen months."

Resigning myself, I admitted, "I guess I could be interested."

George slapped the table hard enough to rattle my wine glass. "Way to seize an opportunity."

I grumbled something grouchy.

"Sorry, didn't catch that."

"Thanks," I said loud enough to be heard.

I would soon learn that my first instinct was the hands-down winner.

Chapter 5

"IT WAS A FIX-UP!" I said aloud, largely to underscore my own amazement. "What do you think of that?"

Bound to happen, babe.

After I finished wiping off my borrowed mascara, I slipped into one of Rip's old t-shirts and a pair of his knit boxers. Fideaux was already asleep on his former master's pillow. I plumped up mine then wriggled under the covers.

Still savoring my evening out, I replayed some of George Whatizname's lame attempts at conversation. Benign, most of it. Almost sadly ordinary. Yet his gut reaction to his son-in-law had secured my attention, albeit not in a good way.

Then he'd gone and asked me to babysit his grandson.

Me. Babysit!

It might be fun.

More and more Rip was sounding like a Monday morning quarterback. However, he had a point. He always did.

I pulled the sheet over my shoulder and turned onto my side.

Precisely eight hours later I sat up and stretched, eager as always to do something. *Anything.* Even babysit, if it came to that.

By seven-thirty I'd dressed in work clothes, packed a lunch, and driven Fideaux to the nearby woods for his daily exercise. Although it was still early, a Jeep I didn't recognize took up half the shallow parking strip on the eastern border of the park. A little disappointing, but chances were good we wouldn't cross paths with the owner and his or her dog—or dogs—in the two-hundred acre forest. Nothing against people in general; I just find nature more restorative when I have it to myself.

Twenty yards in I released Fideaux and we set off at our usual speeds—me, a steady stride, he in his preferred lag-behind/run-ahead pattern. With little breeze to disturb the morning haze, the woods could have been a calendar photograph. Tall oaks, maples, and beeches blotted out most of the sun and discouraged undergrowth, so the eye-level view was mostly tree trunks and the litter of last year's leaves. Designated paths led uphill or down, following either the contour of the land or a shallow creek lined with multi-colored pebbles. Squirrels, chipmunks and deer lived here, also a Great Horned Owl, much to the dismay of the chipmunks. None of the above were in sight this morning, however, and the stillness reminded me of a Hollywood soundstage.

While Fideaux was off sniffing an interesting hole in the ground, I draped his short green leash around my neck. It occurred to me that I shouldn't be so accommodating to a potential attacker, but although Rip's death had made me more cautious in some respects, it had made me lax in others.

Just past the first turn, a German Shorthaired bounced toward us. Not quite keeping pace was a man with receding blonde curls and black-rimmed glasses. He seemed older, but not *old*. Probably still a full-time member of the workforce, judging by the hour he'd chosen to walk his dog. I noted pursed, baby-like lips and drooping shoulders when The Hunter, as I mentally dubbed him, stopped to admire Fideaux.

"What breed?"

"American," I answered, as usual.

"American?"

"Melting pot..."

"Got it. You come here often?" That old chestnut.

"Once in a while. When I have time." So what if the man had been dressed by Nordstroms and owned a not-inexpensive hunting dog; we were alone in the middle of a very large woods. I wasn't about to give him my schedule.

"I just moved here from New York." He smiled as he glanced around. "Beautiful place you've got here."

"Yes," I agreed. So slick.

Much to my dismay, the smile was now aimed at me.

A silence developed, and I noticed those pink lips twitch. At my expense.

Was I suddenly giving out "single" signals? And why did my cheeks feel so hot?

The dogs had finally completed their get-acquainted circle, so I waved Fideaux on ahead. "Have a good day," I told The Hunter over my shoulder.

"Until we meet again…"

Yeah, right.

When both man and dog were out of sight, I said it out loud. "Been there. Done that."

Fideaux appeared to be relieved.

***

BY ELEVEN A.M. I'd begun to see phantoms in the gray, faux-fieldstone tiles the way you see whales and pumpkin heads in the clouds. The majority of the kids' kitchen floor was done; only the tedious edges where every tile required its own paper pattern remained. Using the waxed paper peeled off the last square, I traced the needed shape onto the next piece. Then I cut the soft vinyl with scissors and hoped for the best. All while my bored brain screamed like a caged monkey.

The day was sunny but moderate, so I opened a side window and the door to the outside. The screened door would keep Fideaux in.

Now, along with the expected sounds of trash trucks, birdcalls, and distant traffic came the strident, I-need-mommy wail of a young baby. I shut my eyes and let the precious memories flow.

I was reliving the first day we brought Chelsea home when the real-life crying escalated. Next came a thump, and the distressing wails abruptly stopped.

My skin went clammy. I didn't like any of the scenarios my imagination conjured up, and the frontrunner I *really* didn't like.

Did I dare invent some pretext to find out if the baby was safe? It was the Mrs. Zumstein dilemma all over again, and Chapter #476 in the Mother-in-Law's Manual warned against calling the cops unless I was absolutely one hundred percent certain a crime had been committed in Chelsea and Bobby's neighborhood. If I happened to be wrong, the newlyweds would be forced to live fifteen feet from the family I'd alienated for however long they owned their respective houses. For that *I would not be forgiven*—not by my daughter or her husband. Not by myself, either.

I gritted my teeth and peeled wax paper off another tile.

***

MOTHERHOOD WAS NOT at all what Cissie Voight had imagined. As advertised, she adored her daughter Caroline more than anything else in the world. If anything, that portion of the hype had fallen short of reality. Her daughter's little baby hands, the perfect blonde eyelashes, even the brief gas-induced smiles (hints of the real deal yet to come)—

everything about the child warmed Cissie's heart. Sometimes she worried that she loved her baby too much.

What she didn't care for was everything else. Nothing was easy anymore. Not grocery shopping, cooking dinner, or watching a sitcom. Not even making love with her husband.

As she paired little socks on the coffee table, the baby in her musical swing, she reflected on the couples' counseling session she and Ronald had attended at her church. Five young married couples sat in a circle while the minister coaxed uncomfortable confessions from the men, mostly in response to their wives' complaints. Clearly, every couple was messed up; but it didn't take long to realize she and Ronald were messed up the worst. *Compromise*, the minister emphasized over and over again, usually while looking straight at Ronald.

As if that was ever going to happen with him.

Talk, talk, and more pointless talk, and then a siren went off half a block away. Everybody in the room jumped, but one man actually vaulted over the back of his chair and ran. The next second he was gone.

"Volunteer fireman," his wife explained.

For Cissie, being a mother was like that.

As if to prove the point, Caroline spit up all over her new outfit.

"Perfect," Cissie murmured as she lifted the infant out of the swing.

A building inspector working dusty, dirty construction sites all day, when Ron arrived home, he expected his wife to be panting for a kiss and Shalimar perfume competing with the aroma of roast beef. That hadn't happened since the baby's birth, but Cissie tried every day.

And failed every day.

While she finished snapping up Caroline's clean onesie, she debated whether to ask the woman she'd seen using a saw next door for help. Since she didn't use sawhorses or wear a tool belt or anything, Cissie figured her for one of those do-it-yourself types. She also heard the woman swear when she made a mistake, and a professional wouldn't make that many mistakes. So probably a relative of the newlyweds. Best guess—Chelsea or Bobby's kooky mother.

So maybe she would like to practice being a *grand*mother. Just long enough for Cissie to get a shower, wash her hair, shave her legs. Bliss!

A delicate knock at her backdoor caused her heart to leap and her eyes to check on the baby. Lying in her downstairs Pack N Play, Caroline was still making adorable sucky-faces in her sleep.

Cissie tiptoed to the backdoor anyway.

Standing at the bottom of the steps was the kooky carpenter-woman. Up close she did resemble Chelsea, but shorter; and unlike her neighbor's wavy reddish bob, this woman's cinnamon-colored hair was cropped like a pixie.

Wrapped in a paper towel, her bloody right hand was cradled by her left.

"By any chance do you have an extra band-aid?" she asked.

Chapter 6

"OOH, COME IN," Chelsea's neighbor to the right urged.

I proceeded up the two steps and into a vintage kitchen, circa 1950. At least I thought it would be the fifties style if I could see past the clutter. No dishwasher, which explained the tower of white plates on the drain board. Red-checkered curtains, perhaps fashioned from dish towels. A chipped porcelain table surrounded by chrome and vinyl chairs. Their owner offered me one, then pulled another close for herself.

"What happened?" the young mother asked with a furrowed brow. Her pale blonde hair had been hastily confined by the sort of thick blue rubber bands you find on celery, and she wore dirty jeans and a t-shirt that was damp in the front.

"I was cutting one of those do-it-yourself floor tiles with scissors, and I accidentally snipped myself."

"Let take a look." She peeked under the bloody paper towel at the half-inch gash across my palm.

"Not too bad. I'm Cissie Voight, by the way."

I gave her my name and told her I was Chelsea's mother.

"I already guessed that. Sit still," she said, patting the air. "I'll get some stuff."

She disappeared upstairs, giving me my chance to check the adjacent rooms. Around the corner in the living room a portable crib/playpen contained a baby of about four months. Judging by the pink onesie and lacy socks, it was a girl— peacefully asleep, thank goodness.

Cissie tiptoed downstairs and caught me admiring her child. "That's my little Caroline," she said, flushing with pride.

"Bet you don't know what you did without her."

"Oh, I know what I did, I just can't do it now." Chagrin crossed the new mother's face but quickly fled. "Let's get your hand cleaned up. I've gotta start dinner soon."

Two minutes later my cut was disinfected and protected by a large band-aid.

"You changed your clothes," Cissie observed. Then, noting my surprise added, "I saw you earlier with your dog."

"Oh, right. I brought a clean outfit in case I ran out of tiles, which I did, of course. Home Depot here I come. Again."

Cissie contemplated the crossed hands on her lap. When at last she fixed her gaze on me, I knew she'd come to some sort of decision.

"Ron's always telling me to be more careful, that there are bad people out there, but…" She gave me a blink of a smile, "…but I don't think you're one of them. Do you have to go to Home Depot right away?"

"I guess not. Why? What do you need?"

"I need twenty minutes to take a shower. All you'd have to do is watch Caroline while I'm upstairs. She isn't even awake. I wouldn't ask, but I'm kinda desperate."

That I could see for myself. This woman hadn't had half an hour to herself in at least a week. "Be glad to help. When my kids were new, we ate frozen dinners for months."

Cissie rolled her eyes. "Ronald would kill me if he had to eat that crap."

People exaggerate their spouse's eccentricities all the time; it's almost a sport. But afterwards their lips don't usually tremble or their eyelashes fill with tears. I yearned to reach over and brush the corn silk hair away from the young woman's cheeks, find her a tissue, give her a great big maternal hug.

Instead, I slapped my knees, stood, and pulled her up with me. "Let's get you that shower."

"You mean it?"

"Go," I told her in that pseudo-stern voice even toddlers know is fake.

One last giddy glance, and she practically flew up the stairs.

Little Caroline Voight had kicked off her cotton blanket. Her legs were splayed like a rodeo rider, and she wore the aggrieved expression of someone whose favorite sitcom had just been canceled. Entranced, I watched her baby's lips move in and out, in and out, as if she were about to say something.

Wail.

I scooped her up before the second waaaa, and the child's eyes popped open.

Yikes! Who are you? WAAAA.

The rump in my left hand felt damp, so I ignored the crying and reached for the lid of the portable crib, which back in the day used to serve as a changing table. Holding her in place with her one hand, I collected necessities with the other—a new diaper, a wipe, the tube of diaper rash ointment. Offering comforting play-by-play commentary, I freed the baby's legs, untaped the old and put on the new.

Little Caroline quieted down.

"There," I crowed when I finished. "Even easier than do-it-yourself tile."

Caroline blinked damp blonde eyelashes at the ceiling then opened her mouth to fuss.

"Oh no you don't," I warned. "I promised your mom a shower."

Hoisting the ten-pound treasure to my shoulder, I began to sing, walking and bouncing as the words to an old camp song came to me like déjà vu. "A cannibal king, with a big nose ring, fell in love with a dusky ma—ai—d." No longer politically correct, I'm afraid but my innocent audience wouldn't know that for years yet. My own babies had loved the tune. Chelsea, now an accomplished vocalist, pianist, and choral director, had even sung it herself when she got old enough—off-key, in imitation of me.

When I got tired of walking and bouncing, I sat down on the sofa with the baby on my thighs, her impossibly little feet pressed against my stomach.

"What were you crying about so loudly this morning?" I whispered. "And how come you got quiet so fast?"

The young Ms. Voight pressed her lips tight and blinked.

And then it all went south again. Hunger this time, I assumed. Lifting the baby to my shoulder, I checked the refrigerator. No bottles. The cabinets—no canisters of formula. Caroline was being nursed, but her mother wasn't yet ready to come downstairs.

"Bring her on up," the mother in question called down when I asked what to do. "Do you mind?"

"No problem."

"Just got my hair dried. Thanks a million. You saved my day."

Cissie relieved me of the frantic baby, settled on a cushioned rocking chair, lifted her fresh blouse, and offered Caroline her four-o'clock snack.

Trying not to watch, I scanned the rest of the room. Aqua and yellow gingham here and there, a changing table loaded with blankets and towels, and beside it on the floor a Price Club sized box of generic disposable diapers, one end deeply dented as if it had been dropped. The source of the thump perhaps?

"I couldn't get her to quiet down," I confessed mostly for something to say. "I tried, but she knew I wasn't you."

"Don't worry about it. When she won't settle down for me, I just give her a Binkie."

"Binkie?"

"Pacifier."

"Oh, right." I'd forgotten about them. "Next time I'll know." I smiled to seal my offer of additional help, but Cissie was lost in the mommy-zone.

Just as well that she hadn't heard me. Soon I might be watching another child on a paying basis. The twenty minutes with Caroline had made up my mind.

As I followed Fideaux around Chelsea's backyard before heading to Home Depot, I phoned George Whatizname to report that I was willing to talk to his daughter about the job possibility.

"Splendid! I'll let her know and get back to you."

I said, "Fine," although I'd hoped to cut George out of the loop. Darn that Didi. I was not, I repeat, NOT interested in acquiring any new male friends.

No way. Nix. No thank you.

George called back five minutes later.

We agreed to meet at his daughter's house then go out to dinner.

Chapter 7

I HAD JUST enough time to take Fideaux home and feed him, wash my face, add earrings, and change to better-looking flats. Even as I headed out the door, I was kicking myself for agreeing to dinner with George; but I'd been too surprised to remember how to let a man down nicely.

After squeezing the front door latch to make sure it was locked, I crossed my fingers and hoped the evening wouldn't be one big regret.

Two minutes beyond the nearby Dannehower Bridge put me on the Norristown side street where George's daughter lived. I parked in front of some skinny homes built when necessity had favored utility over good taste. Facing these cheek-to-jowl stood four unadorned brick duplexes. Number Six proved to be the left half of one of these.

After crossing the street, I entered the Swenson's tiny front yard through a chain-link gate as off-putting as a drawbridge. The porch railing sported a realtor's sign, but even without it the peeling white paint and absence of personalization told me the property was a rental.

George opened the door to my knock. He seemed taller somehow, his eyes a livelier golden brown. Could he possibly have more hair than he had at Didi's?

I must not have been paying attention.

"Come in. Come in," he offered, smiling as if he owned the place.

"This is my daughter, Susan." He nodded toward a woman of about thirty with elaborate makeup and chin-length, perfectly straight auburn hair. Her clothing was all black, and her acrylic nails looked as if they could open a soda can.

"…and this is little Jack." George beamed at the toddler kneeling at the coffee table scribbling on a piece of newspaper. He was a beautiful boy, really, with a perky nose centered in a photo-perfect face.

The mother ruffled his blonde curls and urged him to say hello, but the child's concentration never wavered.

"He talks?" I asked. "I thought he was only eighteen months."

"He says some things. When he wants to," Susan replied with a shrug.

"Normal kid."

"Pretty much," she agreed.

"Have a seat." George gestured me onto a soft, blue chair before joining his daughter on the sofa.

"Do you have any experience babysitting?" Susan inquired, "…if you don't mind my asking."

"No, it's a perfectly good question, and the answer is yes and no. I've raised my own two kids, of course, and I changed a diaper a couple hours ago, but I didn't give any thought to babysitting for anyone until your father mentioned it."

"So you don't have any references."

"Her husband was head of a school," George contributed. "They're good people, honey. Why don't we give her a few minutes with Jack, just to see how they get along?"

Susan opened her lips as if to protest then abruptly changed her mind. "Fine," she said. "We'll wait in the kitchen."

After Susan and George departed, Jack spared me a bashful glance that conveyed the hint of a quiet intelligence. Very soon he would be learning things at warp speed. Did I want to be around to watch? Tempting, but not overly so. Of the two of us Rip had been the one soft on all children; I mostly loved my own.

Of course that was then and this was now. Now Garry needed spending money, which I wanted to send freely. "A penny saved is a penny earned," said Ben Franklin, and I'd begun to appreciate exactly what he meant.

I slipped down to sit on the floor, selected a red crayon from the box, and helped myself to a sheet of newspaper. After coloring the truck in a Toyota ad, I offered to trade colors with Jack. "Want this one?"

He accepted the red and relinquished the purple.

Then the front door opened and Daddy Mike swept in.

"Hey, little buddy. Whatcha doing there?"

"Daddy!" Jack threw himself at his father's legs.

The man narrowed his eyes at me. "And who are you, may I ask?"

I rose to my full height, far short of the man's prying gaze. "Ginger Barnes." I extended my hand, but Mike Swenson ignored it.

"Sorry, but you haven't said why you're here."

"I'm an invited guest," I told him, "a mistake that can be remedied at once if your attitude doesn't change."

"Michael!" The voice was Susan's, and judging by her husband's reaction it was uncharacteristically forceful. "This is the babysitter Dad met the other night. We talked about this, remember? If I'm going to take that job, we need somebody to watch Jack."

Swenson glanced down at his son, who was staring back with shock bordering on fear. Not emotions you want a toddler to endure for long, if ever, so I instinctively scooped him into my arms.

Whereupon the father grabbed his wife's bicep and steered her back toward the rear of the house.

"You know what I said about that job," he snarled in a stage whisper. "I can't believe you..."

"We need..." was all I heard of Susan's reply.

Emerging from the wings, George rushed to relieve me of the now-whimpering Jack, who tucked his head under his grandfather's chin and clung to him like lint.

Back in the kitchen the couple continued at a less-than-discreet volume. Most of their words were unintelligible, but their differences were clear. Susan was prepared to go earn money for the greater good. Mike wanted her at home. Macho bluster, in my opinion, but not really my business. I just felt bad that my presence had touched off this particular installment of their argument.

"Sorry about that," George apologized as he petted Jack's curly head. "Let's give them a minute, then I'll hand off Jackie-boy and we can go eat."

"I don't think..." I began, but George showed me his palm.

"You've come out of your way. The least I can do is buy you dinner."

"But I'm leaving," I said. "Right now."

"Understood. How about Sullivan's in fifteen minutes?"

I knew perfectly well what I should have said, but looking into those sorry, insurance-salesman eyes all I could say was, "Fine."

Chapter 8

SULLIVAN'S SAT ON the Route 202 edge of a parking lot for the large, land-locked King of Prussia Mall. Hundreds of people passed by the upscale steak house each day because of its location, location, location—the calculated convergence of four major Pennsylvania roadways. As I stepped into the reception area, I wished I'd had the presence of mind to suggest a less extravagant venue, but I'd been too annoyed with Mike Swenson to think that fast.

George hurried up behind me as I approached the hostess's dais.

"Thanks," he said breathlessly. "Thanks for waiting."

"Just got here myself," I assured him. "Thanks for the invitation."

As we followed the swishing hips of the hostess to a far table, I instinctively secured my shoulder bag between both hands to keep from bumping anything—a person, a slender goblet, a graceful black chair.

"I'm sorry about Mike," George apologized after we'd settled into our seats. "He's…he's…"

"Overbearing?" No reason not to be honest. George had witnessed my reaction to his son-in-law, and he'd already expressed his own doubts about the man.

Musing, he sipped at his water before he responded.

"Protective, I think. Or maybe you're right. I don't know him as well as I'd like. He and Susan met when she was a freshman at Michigan State, and they married there the next year. She left school during her junior year when George took a job out of state. Soon after that they adopted Jack, so…" He shrugged away his daughter's education.

"Has Susan ever worked outside the home?"

"Oh, yes," her father responded perhaps too quickly. "But temporary jobs. Macy's at Christmas, a card-store clerk for a while. She likes doctors' offices, probably because she's visited so many."

Trouble getting pregnant? I wondered because of the adoption.

"Allergies," George offered, his eyes briefly avoiding mine. "Not much of a resume, I know. Which is probably why she's so eager to take this new job—to get a sense of herself, I think. To find out whether she can hack it out there in the business world."

I understood. Why else had I secretly embraced the "Problem Solver" title Didi had bestowed that night so long ago? "Wife" and "Mother" were certainly enviable and worthwhile roles, but more often than not they fell short of describing the whole woman.

"Do you think Mike will talk Susan out of taking the job?"

George shrugged. "I left in a hurry."

"We both did."

When he chuckled in response to my laugh, his cheeks creased in a pleasing pattern, as if he'd done a lot of smiling over the years. Yet his face also looked as if something were missing. Glasses perhaps? Had he had cataract surgery, or maybe lasix?

Best not to ask, I'd learned from Rip, and the thought of my late husband gave me a pang. Here I was dining alone with another man. Something I'd done…never, since I'd lost Rip.

"What are your interests, George?" I asked, the line that had rescued many an uncomfortable silence.

"Ah," George replied with a wince. "That's a tough one."

"How so?"

"I've been a workaholic so long I don't know anything else."

"So you must love your job."

"Selling insurance?"

"Yes. What do you like about it?"

Our drinks arrived, and George used the interruption to contemplate his answer.

"Meeting people," he concluded. "Hearing about their lives. Helping them plan for any eventuality."

"You sound like the Catcher in the Rye." Saving strangers from whatever might go awry. Classic soft-hearted, sophomoric stuff, unless you actually did it for real.

"And you sound like a shrink," he said with a bemused grin.

I sipped my wine while I gave that some thought. "My grandmother was a very wise woman," I said. "Somehow she looked past your skin straight through to your heart. It was amazing, really. I always wished I could be like her."

George shook his head in wonder. "Holden Caufield, the guy who wanted to save everybody." He waved his head again and huffed. "Nobody ever got me so quickly. Certainly not my ex-wife, that's for sure. And you did it inside a minute. You *are* a wise woman, Gin. Don't let anybody tell you otherwise."

Too intense. And too flattering. "Holden Caufield and Pollyanna," I joked.

"No, no," George disagreed. "Cassandra. Wasn't she a seer, or a mind reader, or something?"

"If you say so."

We moved onto trivia, widely skirting his divorce and Rip's demise, Susan and Mike, and anything else of importance for the remainder of the meal. I enjoyed my wine and the medium-rare steak and even the calorie-dense garlic mashed potatoes.

After George's credit card and the bill had been collected, he turned serious. "If Susan wins the argument, will you take the job?"

"Unlikely."

"Unlikely that she'll win, or unlikely that you'll help them out?"

I was saved from an immediate reply by George's cell phone. He said hello, listened a moment, answered, "Do my best," then hung up.

"So will you do it?" he asked again.

"Babysit Jack? I don't know..."

"That was Susan," he informed me. "She and Mike had a battle royal—obviously—but she managed to bring him around."

"Good for her."

"One contingency…"

"Oh?"

"She wants you."

"What about Mike?"

"Oh, you'll love this." George slipped me a sly smile. "He told Susan you're part of the deal."

"How so?"

"It's you or nobody."

I couldn't believe my ears. The officious bastard was confident I would say no, and he would get his way after all.

I withheld the four-letter word on the tip of my tongue.

Babysitters don't talk like that.

Chapter 9

IN SPITE OF the Swenson's ultimatum I told George, "No, I don't think so," regarding the babysitting question.

"Please," George said. "Take a day to think about it." No begging or cajoling, just a reasonable request delivered with dignity and hope.

"How about if I call Susan tomorrow night?" My answer probably wouldn't change, but at least George could report that he'd done his best.

"Thank you," he told me with a small smile.

In the parking lot I thanked him in return for the luxurious dinner and for being patient with me.

Then I hurried on home to Fideaux.

Our nighttime routine began with a prowl around the yard in the dark. While he patrolled the perimeter for raccoons and deer, I enjoyed the fireflies and stars and listened to crickets and owls and distant traffic, all of which helped to pinpoint my miniscule place in the universe.

In the morning I was back at my daughter's by eight. A benign cloud cover held the temperature to a comfortable sixty-nine, so I attached Fideaux's long leash to the huge oak by the side of the yard where he could play sphinx until it was time to nap.

"Water coming right up," I told him. The house had an outside faucet on the suspicious side, the side with the falling trash bags and explosions. When I looked up from filling Fideaux's borrowed bowl, I encountered the scowling countenance of the neighbor in question. Never mind that Mrs. Zumstein remained firmly on her own side of the fence, her expression was right in my face.

"You talk to your dog?" A transparent haze of colorless hair exposed the shape of the tiny woman's skull while sagging puffs of flesh made her appear to be melting.

"Sometimes," I admitted.

"Sign of insanity, you know."

Or loneliness, I might have argued, but I didn't. *Or maybe I just have an affection for animals, how about that?*

She sent a sneering glance over her shoulder before turning back toward her dingy house.

"Sometimes he answers back," I called after her, but Mrs. Zumstein didn't appear to hear. She was switching a coil of clothesline from her right hand to her left in order to pull at her sticky door.

Was that a noose on one end? I wondered, shuddering at the thought. Whatever the woman was up to, it certainly wasn't normal...*and you think I'm crazy?*

The creepiness of Mrs. Zumstein's noose and the loneliness nerve she'd inadvertently exposed haunted me most of the morning. Yet when I went to relieve Fideaux from the escalating midday heat, the neighboring house looked so ordinary and harmless I convinced myself to focus on something else, specifically whether or not to help Susan Swenson find herself.

I still hadn't decided when I put down the last tile and stood to admire my work. I confess it wasn't lost on me that Susan Swenson was yearning for the same sort of satisfaction—with the added incentive of cash, a bonus that would also be mine if I accepted the babysitting job.

By three-thirty I'd put my tools away, swept the floor spotless, and deposited my trash outside in the proper can.

From the open window above me I could hear that baby Caroline was well into her afternoon wail.

Why not? I decided.

Rounding the thick hedge that separated the houses, I tapped on the Voight's front door, and in short order Cissie greeted me with the howling baby propped against her shoulder.

"Ms. Barnes! What a nice surprise."

"I've got some time to kill. How about if I take Caroline for a walk?"

"You serious? That'd be great. You sure? I mean..."

"I'm sure."

The young mother couldn't retrieve the stroller fast enough. Stored in a corner of the entrance hall, it opened with a jerk of the wrist. While Cissie settled the squalling child and fastened straps, she vented her exasperation.

"It's just her fussy time, I guess. I've tried everything— food, diaper, music, the Binkie, her swing. Nothing seems to help. You don't think she's sick, do you?"

I touched the baby's red face, pressed her stomach. No change in the crying. "I don't think so," I concluded. "Some kids just get overtired. I know mine did. Tough to settle them down then."

"You think?"

"Why don't you do something for yourself while we're gone? If she's still crying when we get back, then you can call her doctor."

"Sure," Cissie said, but her wrinkled forehead said otherwise. "You won't be gone long, right?"

"Half an hour. A little longer if she settles down. Deal?"

"Deal."

Baby Caroline fell asleep before the middle of the next block, so I ventured only as far as the small park down the street and flopped gratefully onto a bench. For forty minutes I watched the sun dapple the dancing leaves of the pin oaks above and the three children using the swing set in the corner by the creek. Passing by as they left, their mother said 'hi' and nodded.

I smiled and nodded back. Had we been alone on a city street, the greeting probably wouldn't have occurred. But women with children, even children not their own, shared a mutual bond.

Which brought Susan Swenson to mind again in a different way. Something seemed off about her interactions with Jack. I wondered if the husband demanded so much of her attention that precious little could be spared for the child. Or maybe it had nothing to do with the father and everything to do with Susan herself. Those long nails and perfect coif, impractical to say the least. I had watched the family interact too briefly to guess what was wrong, but what I'd seen made me curious, and when I get curious...

No. I'd been insulted. Demeaned. I didn't need people like that no matter how much they might need me. It was summer. Surely a hundred college students would apply for the job I intended to turn down. The Swensons would have three whole months to look for a permanent sitter.

I glanced at my watch. Time to go back before Cissie began to think I'd kidnapped her daughter.

She greeted me warmly at the door.

"Overly tired," I confirmed, regarding the baby's crying jag.

"Phew." Cissie playfully brushed her brow with her hand. "Now I know. Thanks a million."

I explained that I'd finished working at Chelsea's and wouldn't be around for a while. "But for sure I'll say hello when I'm here. Okay?"

That earned me a hug around the neck and a kiss on my cheek. Women with children; members of the same club.

My own heart did a little giddyup when I saw my own daughter's car in the drive.

"Mom! It looks gorgeous," she effused as I entered the backdoor. "Thank you so much."

"Glad you like it." *Glad* was only half of how I felt. *Relieved* was the other.

"Like it? I love it. Bobby will, too."

"Let's hope."

We carried glasses of iced tea into the living room and settled down for a chat.

"How was your day?" I inquired, which prompted a litany of the issues and deadlines that plague teachers at the end of the school year.

"By the way," I remarked when Chelsea finished. "Mrs. Zumstein thinks I'm crazy."

The left corner of Chelsea's lips lifted. "Takes one to know one."

I gave that the grunt it deserved. Then I mentioned that I'd also met Cissie Voight. "What's her husband like?"

"An asshole," my daughter declared without an instant's thought. "I swear he mows his grass when you're having a cookout—on purpose. Then when *he* has company, he parks so nobody can get into our drive." She waved her head. "I don't know how Cissie can stand him."

Not exactly what I'd been hoping to hear. "Maybe you can be nice to her now and then."

Chelsea shot me that look. "In my spare time?"

"Speaking of spare time…" I described the babysitting job offer and Susan Swenson's dilemma.

"Reminds me of some Dad's Bryn Derwyn families. And mine," Chelsea observed. "Messed up parents; messed up kids."

I couldn't argue with that.

"You'd be great with Jack," Chelsea concluded, "but do you really want the job?"

I lifted my eyes from the spot I'd been staring past and stated what I thought was the truth.

Yes," I said. "I believe I do."

Chapter 10

ON MONDAY MORNING Susan Swenson greeted me like a kid with the keys to the candy store—flushed face, irrepressible grin.

"You're on time," she trilled with wide-eyed surprise, right away a not-so-good sign. Wasn't being on time pretty much the first rule of gainful employment?

Nervous. She was probably just nervous, but now I was, too.

"You look nice." I made the bland remark to settle us both down. Anyhow, Susan's outfit did flatter her slim figure, and the black and white combination looked businesslike.

"You think so?" Fishing for praise, but forgivable under the circumstances. How could she be anything but insecure married to Mr. Wives-Belong-At-Home Mike?

"Great first impression," I assured her.

Susan's eyebrows lowered with concern. "The problem is it's the only outfit I've got. Any chance you can stay a couple hours longer so I can shop?"

I didn't want to disappoint the woman, but I didn't want her to think I was a doormat either. I compromised and said I hoped to be home by three.

"Sure. Absolutely. Whatever you say."

"So where's little Jack?"

"Oh! Kitchen." She waved a hand toward the back of the house.

Strapped into his high chair, the toddler grinned mischievously then slammed his tray and sprayed Cheerios in a five-foot radius.

"Hiya, Jack" I greeted him. "Aren't you cute?"

He swept the tray with his arm, sending more cereal, applesauce, and milk flying.

"Really cute."

Susan slipped into the kitchen to hand me a computer printout of her child's routine. The list extended well into the afternoon, suggesting that Mommy had anticipated a positive answer to her shopping request. *Hoped for*, I corrected myself giving her the benefit of a doubt. Still…

Susan spun on her heel as if preparing to leave.

"Don't forget to give me Jack's car seat," I called after her.

She spun back. "Why?"

Why?

"So he'll be safe if I have to take him anywhere?"

Or just to go someplace more stimulating than this house, I might have added. There was no space for Jack to run outside, and frankly the Swenson's home depressed me. The blank walls and unadorned windows. The lack of throw pillows or knickknacks. No magazines or books, just a heap of plastic toys in the corner of the living room, a sofa, two chairs, and a TV. The dining room offered a table and four chairs, one plant on the windowsill, and a changing pad on top of a short file cabinet. All in all the impression was of an unloved home, or a temporary home, or a bare-bones home because there was no money. No matter which description fit, I didn't see myself spending all of my Monday, Wednesday, and Friday mornings stuck here. It certainly wouldn't do Jack much good either.

"Okay." Susan nodded with finality. "Bye," she said over her shoulder as she pulled the front door shut with those manicured fingers.

I opened it again. "Car seat, Susan! And how about a door key?"

She barked out a nervous giggle. Then she extracted the seat from her car and danced it to me with an eye-roll at her own expense.

"Key?" I repeated.

A key was swiftly retrieved from a drawer, and Susan was swiftly gone.

When I returned to unharness Jack from his high chair, he was yelling "Mama" and crying as if his heart would break.

I carried the squirming boy to the sink, wiped the applesauce from his face and hands, then set him on his feet.

Zoom, he was through the dining room and into the living room. "Mama," he cried as he pounded his fists on the front door.

"A cannibal king," I sang as I sidled up to him, "with a big nose ring..."

"Mama!"

I chose to let the kid cry it out. I was a stranger, after all, and should expect to be distrusted.

Meanwhile, I dug out the crayons Jack had been using when we met and began to draw circles on yesterday's newspaper. I hummed my song, too, because now the tune was in my head.

When Jack finally flopped on the floor beside me, I thought I heard a squish. Breakfast, milk, diaper. That had been the routine of every child I ever met.

"Are you wet?" I asked.

Blank stare.

"Want a new diaper?" The toddler was probably old enough to realize when he needed changing. Maybe Susan had begun to point it out.

Nothing.

"Okay, buddy. We have to start somewhere." I scooped him off the floor. "Dang, you're heavy." After depositing him on the changing pad in the dining room, I removed the soggy diaper.

"Wet," I told him pointedly, holding up the evidence.

"Now you say it—wet. Oooh et." Although I seemed to have his attention, what I got was another blank stare.

After playing at home for a while, I took him to Petco to buy dog food for Fideaux. Jack loved the parakeets and kittens but seemed especially entranced by a cage full of ferrets. When that novelty wore off, he ran the aisles like a cyclist biking the hills of France.

I lumbered along like a support-vehicle low on gas. In desperation I lunged and finally caught him. He squirmed and giggled in my arms.

Good, I thought. Now we're having fun.

At naptime Jack slept like a hibernating bear while I watched my favorite HGTV show with drooping eyelids.

Three o'clock came and went without Susan.

At three-thirty I began to worry.

At four I began to fume.

Susan breezed in at four-twenty. "Oh, what a day," she said, angling shopping bags through the doorway.

I didn't say a thing.

"…The job is great. I love the people, and you should see what I bought."

"I really can't," I told her. "You said you'd be back by three."

Susan blushed. "I'm sorry. I thought it would be okay."

We shared a weighty stare, then she waved away the awkwardness. "How was Jack anyway? Any problems?"

"None," I replied. At lunchtime he'd spit carrots on himself and also on me, but that wasn't worth mentioning.

What did concern me was Susan, her eagerness to escape, her reluctance to return. It was too early to make much of it, but I was uncomfortable with our beginning.

***

WHEN I FINALLY arrived home, a strange man stepped out of the shadow of my front door stoop.

Chapter 11

WHERE I LIVE strange men rarely show up on one's doorstep, maybe a pair of religious recruiters once a year, or a guy running for school board every four. For one thing, we have no sidewalks and some of our driveways only a Mountain Goat could love. Girl Scouts don't even venture down Beech Tree Lane during cookie season.

So, naturally, I was wary of the man with the clipboard.

He stood about five-ten and had the rounded edges of middle age, but just because he looked marshmallowy did not mean he was soft.

"Ms. Barnes?" he addressed me in a predictably saccharine tone. "I'm John Butler from the Census Bureau."

"Oh?" I challenged. I'd been thinking "salesman," but since I'd heard nothing about a census being conducted, "con man" seemed more likely. I selected the front-door key from the bunch in my hand.

"Yes. I need to ask you a few questions. Do you have a few minutes?"

"No, sorry. I don't."

"You were chosen specifically to represent this area. Can you suggest a better time?"

How about never! "I'm not comfortable giving out personal information. Can't you interview someone else?"

"Not really. It won't take..."

I knew Fideaux often napped in the front hall while I was away, so I deliberately dropped my purse. His startled response was loud enough to induce a heart attack.

"Good-bye, Mr. Butler," I told the man as I slipped inside. *Please don't come back.*

I shut the door firmly behind me.

"Good dog," I cooed to my happy pet. "Very good dog. Let's get you a treat."

After dinner, I checked for lurking men before hustling him into the car. Jack had about worn me out, but Fideaux needed to stretch his legs, and a walk in the woods wouldn't hurt me either. At least I hoped not. Just to be safe, I opted for the park's most popular trail along the creek.

While Fideaux trotted a dozen yards uphill to investigate an interesting smell, I thought back on my day. Maybe I should take Jack to the toddlers' story hour at the library, or maybe bring him to play in the creek on a hot day, let him feel a little mud between his toes. I knew of a school jungle-gym that neighbors were free to use when classes were over…

"Charlie! Charlie!" called a male voice as a brown blur sped past my legs. Spotting Fideaux, the blur slowed to a trot. Then a walk. He and Fideaux engaged in the usual sniff routine.

The Hunter, as I'd dubbed the German Shorthaired's owner, came to a breathless halt six feet away.

This was a test, I decided. Would I allow myself to be rattled by every stranger I met simply because one marshmallowy, self-described census taker surprised me on my doorstep? Or would I disown my jitters and behave like my old, intrepid self?

I lingered while The Hunter caught his breath.

"So do you like it here as much as New York?" I inquired.

"My goodness! A friendly question," he remarked with a sardonic smile. "Are you sure you want to risk your status as a true Philadelphian?"

A few of my minor muscles twitched. "Being reserved doesn't mean we're unfriendly."

One blond eyebrow arched. "Really?"

I've always imagined New Yorkers to be smarter, wittier, more worldly, and more ruthless than those who chose Philadelphia as their home, generalizations that are probably no truer than the perception that Philadelphians are slow to accept strangers. His choice of dog aside, had I labeled this stranger unfairly?

Or was it my protective instincts again?

I once read that a male police detective preferred a female partner, "because women are more aware of their surroundings," historically because we needed to be.

Forget about why I had the jitters. Surrounded by shadows rapidly blurring the landscape, I voted for instinct.

"We better keep moving," I remarked.

"Don't let me stop you," the man in the Buddy Holly glasses complained as he signaled his dog to proceed.

Dilemma. If I obeyed my nervous system, I'd be tramping on the Hunter's heels all the way back to my car.

Instead I gritted my teeth, secured Fideaux's attention with two pats to my leg, and proceeded deeper into the woods. The stretch ahead seemed clear for thirty yards. Beyond that I couldn't say.

Nightfall came on fast. I clicked on my phone's flashlight app to keep from tripping.

Sensing my fear, Fideaux lifted his ears, and pranced on his toes as if poised to bolt. When an owl's hoot sent chills up my arms, I caved in and turned around.

Now I couldn't reach my car fast enough, couldn't wait to secure me and my skittish pet inside something that felt like a fortress.

Thirty yards uphill.

Twenty.

Ten.

I clicked the unlock button on the Acura's remote. The lights blinked in response.

I allowed myself to breathe.

Chapter 12

NO BOOGEYMEN jumped from behind the bushes when Fideaux and I raced to our front door; but once inside I turned on lights I didn't need, locked up extra tight, and poured myself a small brandy.

Curled up on the sofa, my companion at my feet, I longed to call my son, but I resisted. Garry would be consumed by whatever nineteen-year-olds did on vacation on Cape Cod, and I doubted that he would welcome an interruption from his mother.

Instead I scanned the living room for the book I was into, which made me notice that I had a phone message.

"Mom, give me a call, will you?" Chelsea requested with a hint of panic.

"What's up?" I asked as soon as we connected.

"My mother-in-law is coming to visit."

A relieved laugh burst out of me. "Without her husband?" An executive of some sort, all I knew for certain was that Chelsea's father-in-law traveled for work.

"Seattle," she explained. "Mom! What am I going to do with Marilyn?" Marilyn Alcott, not "Mother Alcott" or "Bobby's mother," or God forbid, "Mom," which I hoped would forever refer only to me.

"Valley Forge? The Phillies? How should I know? You'll be done school before she arrives, won't you?"

"Yes, and unlike you, she loves shopping. I'm talking about where she'll sleep. The guest room is stuffed with wedding presents and camping gear."

"Want her to stay with me?"

Chelsea reminded me that I didn't exactly live around the corner.

"Hotel?"

"Heavens no. Totally wrong message."

"Sofa? Oh, right." When I'd stretched out on it, their sectional slid apart and dumped me on the floor.

I finally caught my daughter's drift. The top floor of the kids' ninety-seven-year-old Victorian possessed two unused rooms. As I recall, they contained nothing but stale air, bat poop, and dust.

"How long do we have?"

"Ten days."

"Pick a paint color yet?"

"No, but Marilyn likes blue."

Tuesday wasn't my scheduled day with Jack, and Chelsea's school meeting wasn't until two. We agreed to start early.

No longer lonely, I bent over and gave Fideaux a vigorous belly rub.

"Don't they call bat poop guano, or something?" I asked the dog. "Maybe that's only when they use it for fertilizer.

"Doesn't matter. It won't be fun to clean up even if we call it Chloe and buy it a skirt."

***

FOR UNLOADING purposes I parked as close as possible to Chelsea and Bobby's front door.

Glancing back, I caught sight of a large man in a disreputable bathrobe on Mrs. Zumstein's porch. Something about him made me smile, so I watched as he yawned and ran a meaty hand through his straight, sandy hair. He reached down for the newspaper.

Oops. Nothing on under the robe.

Lucky he didn't notice me. Indeed, his eyes were so puffed up, I wondered whether he'd be able to read the newspaper. A hangover maybe? Was that what Maisie Zumstein did to a person?

Not my problem. I set about trucking my shop vac and the other tools the kids probably wouldn't have into the front foyer.

Chelsea shouted hello as she hammered down the stairs and rushed out the door. "Taking Bobby's wallet to the train station. Have some coffee."

I admired the new kitchen floor as if I hadn't put it there. Then I realized that if I wanted coffee, I would have to make it.

When Chelsea returned, we sat at the breakfast bar.

"So who's the Incredible Hulk next door?" I inquired after we had our day nailed down.

"Incredible Bulk's more like it. Mrs. Zumstein's grandson."

"He her intended victim?"

"Victim?"

I explained about the weird behavior I'd observed, the falling objects, the strange popping noise, and the ensuing smell. The noose, if it had been a noose.

Chelsea shrugged. "I work, Mom. You tell me what's going on. I scarcely know the people."

"You must know something. Like why is the grandson here? Does he have a job?"

"If I had to guess, I'd say he's here because he doesn't have a job."

"There. Was that so hard?"

For mental exercise Chelsea clearly preferred music over speculation, because the first thing she set up on the third floor was a radio. Then came dust masks and trash bags, the shop vac, and hot sudsy water. Before long we both looked like chimney sweeps.

We showered then went to Burger King for lunch. Then Chelsea had that school meeting, so I volunteered to pick up the paint.

After taking it upstairs—two gallons of cornflower blue and white for the woodwork—I opted for a lazy half-hour in the kids' backyard before facing the turnpike.

Fideaux flopped across my borrowed blanket as soon as I spread it on the grass. Scooching him over, I lay watching clouds through the trees and the sky beyond.

Completing the perfection, a beautiful male voice began singing *Ol' Man River*. Had to be a recording, the voice was that professional, that moving. I closed my eyes and let the lyrics break my heart.

"No!" someone shouted from the opposite yard. "NO! Please don't tell me..." Cissie Voight, distraught about something.

Rip often said I would dive into a pond to save a frog. "The fool who rushes in," was another favorite.

This time I believed he would endorse my instinct. As Head of a school, he had encountered plenty of messy marriages. Surely he would agree that Cissie was up to her earlobes in pond water.

I stashed Fideaux back in the house then scurried around the hedge to tap on the Voight's backdoor.

"Anybody home?" I called, discreetly in case the baby was asleep.

The screen door opened inside of three seconds.

"You're back," Cissie exclaimed. "It must be mental telepathy." She wore a stained lavender t-shirt and denim shorts. Without makeup she looked about two.

"No telepathy," I told her. "Just good ears."

"You know anything about cable TV?"

I shrugged a tentative yes.

"Omigosh, where are my manners? Come in."

The kitchen was in disarray again, but judging by the rubber gloves and the sink full of bubbles, Cissie had been trying to do something about it.

"What's the problem?"

She gestured toward the small TV in the corner of the counter. "It comes on, but no programs."

I unplugged the set briefly, but that didn't work. I suggested she call the cable company.

Cissie squeezed her face between her hands. "They keep you on hold forever then ask you to do things I don't understand."

I began to suspect that she needed a backbone more than a soft-hearted volunteer, so I amended my offer. "How about you call the cable people, while I do the dishes. Deal?"

"I guess so. Thanks, Ms. B."

She was still on with Technical Support when Caroline mewed for attention, so I set aside the last wet dish and hurried to rescue the child from her Pack N Play.

When laughter suddenly blared from the TV, Cissie swept back into the kitchen flushed with pride.

She had just relieved me of her squalling baby, when the backdoor squeaked open and closed with a slam.

Mr. Wonderful had come home early.

Chapter 13

BASED ON WHAT Cissie had said about her husband, I already disliked the man. Now here he was, Viking blond and beautiful, masculine with a capital M, flashing a Hollywood smile, and offering to shake my hand. Every man under fifty has tried to bring off the too-busy-to-shave look, but Ronald Voight owned it. His clothing was broken-in and mussed just right, his boots steel-toed and dirty. Not many women would kick this one to the curb.

"Who's this?" He addressed his wife, but his bead on me never wavered.

Cissie had stepped back as soon as her husband entered the house. She stopped biting her lip to answer. "This is Ms. Barnes, Ron honey. Chelsea's mother."

"Cheslea who?"

Cissie's neck suddenly looked scalded. "The new neighbors. You know. Chelsea and Bobby next door."

Trying to be cute, and almost bringing it off, Voight folded his arms and peered at me like a game-show host asking a thirty-thousand dollar question. "And to what do we owe this pleasure?"

Cissie jumped in. "She been a big help, Ron. I had to call the cable company, and, and the TVs working again. You can watch the Phillies if they're on, or whatever..."

Ronald chewed the side of his cheek. "You from around here?"

I mentioned the name of my town, but I couldn't tell if it met with relief or indifference. At the time it didn't seem to matter.

"How was your day?" Cissie asked.

Ronald dropped his arms. Wandered over to the Formica table. Tented his fingers on it. "Same old, same old. What's for dinner?"

"I, I haven't started yet."

"Been busy?"

"Well, yes. The baby, then the TV went out…"

"Um hum." Ronald stepped closer. Wrapped his arms around his wife's head and kissed her hair. The challenging stare he gave me clearly conveyed, "This is private."

As I pulled the backdoor shut, I saw that Cissie had freed her face enough to breathe.

If I had to guess, I'd have said she was in shock.

Chapter 14

AFTER RESCUING Fideaux from my daughter's house, I began the slow, rush-hour drive home. I considered putting on some music, but artificial cheeriness didn't suit my mood. It took a few miles, but I finally figured out what was wrong.

I liked Cissie. She reminded me of me when my first child was little. Back then I yearned to be the Super Woman I thought everyone expected me to be—that *I* expected me to be. How freeing it would have been to have even a half-hour without that pressure.

Was it so wrong to want to give Cissie some relief, to allow her to accomplish one minor chore without interruption, to have some small victory to brag about to her husband?

Having met Ronald, maybe yes.

Just at the sight of him Cissie's confidence appeared to plummet. Then came the "busy" remark, which may have been sympathy but sounded like a dig. Same with the "dinner" question. And then came that smothering hug.

I am not naïve. I know opposites attract. But Cissie and Ronald's match must have been made in Psych 101.

As soon as he saw Cissie had had my help, I saw that my good intentions had backfired.

Again.

***

WEDNESDAY MORNING my woodsy park was softened by mist. Van Gogh might have painted the broad oak trunks in thick strips of black and white, the heavy leaves electric blue drenched in silver. The lace of distant beeches, first to catch the sun, could have been butter yellow with a gentle touch of blue-green. In contrast to yesterday afternoon, my day started with a smile.

Fideaux wanted to linger over what I refer to as his "p-mail," and although I didn't mind his dawdling, I had a job to get to and was forced to hurry him along.

Trying to watch my footing and daydream too, I was startled when another woman rounded the corner from the second bridge. Judging by its bouncy gait, the fluffy tan dog tugging her along was a youngster.

"Creepy in here isn't it?" the stranger remarked. Roughly forty years of age, she wore a tight exercise outfit, matching wristbands, and an unzipped jersey. Probably on her way to spin class and a salad lunch with the girls.

"First time here?" I guessed. Compared to Monday evening the park seemed downright festive.

"Ooh, yeah." Her eyes darted from tree to tree as if she expected an ambush.

She didn't need to know I'd been spooked here, too, so I defended the place. "It'll grow on you, so to speak," I remarked. *Or not.*

The fluff ball pulled hard enough on his leash that the woman waved good-bye.

Fideaux and I soon entered a natural tunnel of saplings. Whether it was the nervous newcomer's misgivings or my own I couldn't say, but a shiver began at my wrists and ran up the back of my neck. I thought Fideaux might offer some protection, *might* being the operative word.

Long ago I'd learned a few self-defense moves, but who knew if I would have the presence of mind to use one of them?

I glanced at my watch.

"Fideaux! Turn around. I have to go to work."

I'd almost forgotten. My time was no longer completely my own.

***

SUSAN SWENSON hurried off to her job with every bit as much glee as the first day, no visible ambivalence at all. Shiny auburn hair flying, eyes flashing, red lips twitching to repress a giggle, she touched my arm and might have hugged me if I'd been a smidgen more inviting.

"Good morning, sport," I addressed the youngster.

Strapped into his high chair nibbling Froot Loops one by one, he eyed me with calculation.

"Di-pur," he said.

"Oh! Are you wet?"

His mischievious grin spread into a devilish smile. He was engaging me in his little game, and I was thrilled.

"You done eating?" I asked. "Are you full?"

Jack's chubby fist swiped cereal to the floor.

Guess so.

Just to be certain, I held Jack's sippy cup of milk to his mouth.

He turned his head.

"Diaper?"

"Di-pur," he repeated.

I released him from the high chair, lifted him with effort, and settled him on my hip. I carried him to the makeshift changing table in the dining room, checked his pants, and announced. "You're dry."

The toddler's eyes twinkled.

Jack—one. Babysitter—zip.

"Dry," I emphasized with a motherly smile. "You're dry," I repeated, thinking to myself *and you know it.*

I encouraged him to play with blocks for a while, letting him alone as long as his attention span lasted. Then I helped him imagine a highway and a truck, a gas station and a grocery store. I pretended his choice was to buy eggs, pickles, beans, or Froot Loops.

"Froo loos," he declared. Whether they were new words or not, I had no clue.

This time when I checked, his diaper was wet.

"Wet," I told him.

"Oo-et," he replied. Whether it meant anything to him or not, again—no clue.

I packed strawberry cereal bars and water for us both, locked the house, then walked Jack and the car seat to my red two-door sedan. I deposited the boy in the far part of the backseat then wrestled with the seat belt until the seat was attached according to regulations. Wondering how young mothers managed to get anything done, I snared the wriggling child, buckled him up, and wiped sweat from my brow.

First stop—the nearest library. A homey old standby, the lower-level children's section possessed a broad view of a tree-dotted lawn. I let Jack romp downhill before capturing his hand and walking him inside. From a table display, I selected a book about trucks with cardboard pages and lots of pictures. Snuggling the child against me on one of the beanbag chairs, I noticed the librarian mirroring my smile.

At the last page, I inquired, "Again? More?" Which word did Jack know?

He closed the book and tried to reopen it at the beginning.

"Again," I taught him. "Again. You say it."

"Gan," Jack replied, and I warmed with déjà vu. How magical it had been teaching my own children, being there when they understood something for the first time, and how lovely it was to experience some of those special moments with Jack. Would Susan be jealous if she knew? I thought not. I felt more empathy coming from the librarian.

After two more 'gans' and two more readings, I selected four additional books and signed them out. Enough static stuff. It was time to turn the boy loose. A municipal park near the high school faced a busy street. Maybe some of the trucks pictured in the library book would drive by.

The park was a grassy, shaded plot with two cannons and a fenced corner with wood chips on the ground. Inside were swings, seesaws, and a jungle gym.

I settled the boy on a bench and produced our snacks. Jack allowed me to feed him bites of the sticky cereal bar; and when that had been washed down, I used the water left in my bottle to rinse my fingers.

"Oo-et," Jack remarked.

My eyes flew open. "Wet. Yes, my fingers are wet," I agreed. Jack not only remembered the word but had used it in a different context, an astonishing degree of comprehension for his age.

"Good boy," I praised him. "Very, very good boy." I grinned my pleasure and gave him a spontaneous kiss. "We're going to have a lot of fun, you and me."

The jungle gym was too large and the seesaws too risky, so I pushed Jack on a red plastic swing seat that resembled a Medieval chastity belt. When he'd had enough, I stood him backwards on the bench next to me and named the types of cars and trucks driving past. *Van, car, panel truck, tanker.*

Suddenly Jack shouted, "Daddy! Daddy, daddy, daddy." He clambered down from the bench and ran to the chain-link fence that ran along the street. "Daddy, daddy, daddy."

Mike Swenson glanced toward the boy before resuming his conversation with another man. Both had emerged from an office building opposite the park. A curbside sign identified it as the "Norristown News."

Probably going to lunch, I decided, since a small shopping center with a few fast food possibilities lay half a block away.

"Daddy!" Jack's sweet voice was filled with hurt, his lashes laden with tears.

Could one daddy-daddy-daddy sound like any other to an adoptive father? It seemed unlikely, but as with Susan, I simply didn't know.

I scooped up my shoulder bag and the whimpering child and headed toward the parking lot.

"He was busy, Jackie," I murmured softly into the boy's ear. "I don't think he heard you."

Yet I didn't believe myself for a minute. Mike had looked straight at his son—and his difficult-to-miss pink-clad babysitter—then deliberately turned away.

All the way to the car the toddler clung to my neck and snuffled against my shoulder. I hugged him and patted his back, but he was still sniffling when I buckled him into his car seat. When I checked him in the rearview mirror a moment later, he was sucking his thumb and staring out the window.

How could anyone hurt a child like that? In my opinion nothing could possibly justify such behavior.

And yet it had happened *on my watch*.

I vowed to find out why.

Chapter 15

"DON'T I EVEN get a cup of coffee?" I joked, knowing full well my daughter had the brushes and roller ready to go.

"Just teasing," I admitted. "Lead the way."

She opted to use the roller first. We would trade when her wrist got tired.

The color looked great, and I reveled in the luxury of spending time with my daughter. Lovely as that was, between the work and the bright, late-June day, the fan Bobby provided soon proved to be inadequate and I caught myself swiping my forehead with a sleeve.

"Hope your mother-in-law isn't a late sleeper," I remarked regarding the summer heat.

Our conversation started out light, but by the time we'd completed the front wall and half of a side it began to touch on the more personal things one mentioned only when the time felt right.

Chelsea asked me if I was lonely.

"Not the way you mean," I answered honestly. "I miss your dad. I'll always miss him, but I don't think I'm ready to date."

"My friend, Corey, told me her mother said she minds not having a witness to her life."

"Heavy," and true. "But I've got you and your brother. And Fideaux, of course."

"And Gramma Cynthia."

"Yes, and Didi."

I chose not to mention that Chelsea had Bobby; Garry had his roommate and a dorm full of fellow freshmen; and

Didi had finally found Will, who so very obviously adored her. Even my mother had remarried a lovely widower with an irresistible laugh. So at the moment Fideaux was the closest thing I had to a life partner. Who else "witnessed" my tiny triumphs and everyday failures? The drawer I finally wrestled open, the grapefruit juice in my eye, the disappointment of no Sunday *New York Times*, the new outfit I wore to the grocery store because I didn't have anywhere better to go. Fideaux observed it all, my private tears included. At those moments he was at my side—heck, in my lap—until I finally had to laugh over his concern.

Two stories down someone knocked on the kitchen door.

Chelsea automatically scanned herself for paint spatters, but since I didn't especially care if I looked like a mess, I offered to go.

"Oh, hi, Mrs. B," Cissie Voight said with obvious delight. "I thought I saw your car."

Then she grimaced and wrung her hands. "I know you're busy, but is there any chance you could do me one more favor?"

Although I did worry about becoming the young woman's crutch, I really *really* disliked Ronald Voight's attitude. Beyond being too chauvinistic for words, he was scary slick, and scary trumped clingy any day. So naturally I said, "Certainly. What do you need?"

Tucking her hyperactive hands under her arms, Cissie explained that Caroline was outgrowing her bassinet, and somehow she needed to assemble their second-hand crib and bring a dresser up from the basement.

"The trouble is I stink at putting things together, and the dresser's too heavy to carry by myself. Since you're really good at stuff like that, I wondered if you'd mind..."

Since I intended to help Chelsea finish her guest room on time no matter what, even if it took me a week of all-nighters, I figured a half-hour break wouldn't make much difference.

"Just let me tell my daughter what I'm doing."

"Thanks, Mrs. B! You're a sweetheart." Cissie reached out to hug me, but I raised my hands.

"Paint," I pointed out. "It's all over me."

Cissie didn't care. The hug was long and enthusiastic.

I thought Chelsea might scold me again for "adoping her whole neighborhood," but instead she said, "You're a nice person, you know that?"

Dumbstruck, I must have stood there a moment too long, because she laughed and told me to, "Go!" with her fingers walking on air. "I know you'll come back; I've got your dog."

Baby Caroline's room had been cleared and cleaned, but this week's fresh clothes remained in their wash basket, and the changing table and accessories were still in the master bedroom with the bassinet.

Crib parts were in a heap on the floor. The spindles appeared to be spaced to current standards, but the finish showed a fair amount of wear. "You can cover those marks with scratch remover, you know," I pointed out. "Not the top edge where Caroline might teethe, but the rest."

"Thanks. I will."

No instructions were available, but assembling a crib wasn't rocket science, and I managed the job in less than fifteen minutes. Together Cissie and I added a rubber pad to the mattress, a soft pink sheet, matching bunny-covered bumpers, and a musical mobile.

"Now about the dresser." A pinch of concern marred Cissie's brow. "It's really heavy."

"Girl power!" I said with an optimistic fist punch.

Unfortunately, I was wrong. Waving my head in surrender, I confessed that we needed a man.

Cissie's face clouded. Clearly, she'd hoped to impress her husband with her resourcefulness.

"Stay right here," I instructed. "I'll be right back."

Mrs. Zumstein's porch leaned left, but its roof sagged right. The screen on the front door was torn, and the flower bed needed a good weeding. In contrast to the summery softness of the surroundings, the old Victorian's battleship hue and maroon trim looked as if Count Dracula had crashed a cookout.

"Is your grandson at home?" I inquired when Maisie herself answered the door. She wore a wool jumper and black ankle boots, both styles I had seen and perhaps even worn but from an era I couldn't quite place.

"Why?" the gnome-like homeowner demanded.

"I need to ask a favor. It's for Mrs. Voight two doors down."

Maisie stared for a couple of blinks then waddled back into the house. Thick shadows prevented me from seeing whether she continued straight out the backdoor.

Yet a moment later the young man I'd seen collecting the newspaper in his bathrobe widened the door opening. "'lo," he said in a friendly manner. "Who're you?"

I explained. "I was wondering if you might be able to help Mrs. Voight and me move a piece of furniture from her basement to her baby's room."

Close up, the fellow looked better than his first impression, and it wasn't just the shorts and golf shirt. The morning's puffiness was gone, revealing eyes the color of blueberries. His lashes were blonder than his straight, sandy hair, his teeth even but slanted so his smile appeared to be crooked.

"You're thinking I played football," he guessed.

"Hadn't thought about it. Did you?"

More smile. "Nope, so I guess you'll have to take the heaviest end."

Cute answer. Cute guy. I liked him.

He stepped onto the porch, headed down the steps.

Cissie met us at the front door, her color warm, her excitement obvious. She looked beautiful.

"Eric Zumstein," my recruit introduced himself, taking her delicate fingers in his meaty paw. From his expression I feared he would lift them to his lips.

"I'm Cissie Voight."

"Pleased ta meetcha. Do you have cats?"

"No."

"Good. I'm allergic as hell. Lead the way."

As we progressed single file down the basement stairs, I remarked, "Your grandmother has cats, I take it?"

"Two, Hanzel and Gretyl. I can deal with them during the day, but Gretyl insists on sleeping with me all night whether I like it or not."

Which explained the puffy eyes I'd attributed to a hangover. "You can't shut your bedroom door?" I wondered aloud.

"What door? I'm sleeping on a foldout in the living room."

The three of us stood facing the dresser, a four-drawer, maple specimen that was taller than it was wide. Surrounding us were miscellaneous boxes and household junk, and a laundry tub adjacent to a washer and dryer.

While gazing at Cissie, Eric rubbed his big paws together. "How about you ladies take a drawer or two and I'll handle the rest?"

"You sure you don't want help?" That was me talking. Cissie was too busy staring back.

"Nope," Eric responded as if Cissie had spoken. "Easier to steer it by myself. Don't want nicks on your walls or bruises on those pretty arms and legs." He handed Cissie the narrowest drawer.

I ended up helping myself.

Cissie led the way with me and my two drawers next. Eric set the last one aside then hefted the whole dresser up the stairs behind us.

"Nice room. Where's the baby?" he inquired when we arrived upstairs.

"Sleeping in my room. *Our* room, Ronald would make me say. He's very possessive." She glanced around as if her husband might jump out of a closet.

"Don't blame him," Eric observed, and another super-charged glance was exchanged.

"I'll just..." *go get the other drawer,* I intended to say, but nobody was listening. I made the trip to the basement and back lickety-split, not because I thought I could stop a rolling train, because I felt responsible for the wreck that appeared imminent.

"Can you stay for lunch?" Cissie addressed her knight-in-shining-armor directly, and anxiety caused me to do something I would not normally have done. I invited myself.

"Oh, thanks," I effused. "I'm ready for a break. Can I contribute something?"

"Uh, no," Cissie replied with heat painting her cheeks. "I've just been to the store."

Eric displayed his crooked grin. "Love to," he told Ronald Voight's beautiful wife.

"Anything to get away from those cats."

Chapter 16

MIKE SWENSON pressed his fingers to his forehead and tried to focus on the want ads he was processing for the newspaper. Mechanics, waiters, sales staff for an electronics store. One for an ETL developer, whatever that was. Nothing for a teacher/football coach, which he once was but could no longer be. Instead he had accumulated his very own list of brainless, dead-end jobs, work scarcely rewarding enough to put food on the table.

For relief, his eyes strayed to the photograph on his desk. Leaning against his beloved silver Audi, arms extended to show off her new son, Susan wore that blousy yellow-print dress she thought made her look "motherly." The photo always reminded him of the car's imminent departure and the large payment he received, which served to underscore a hard-earned lesson. *Family above all.* No one could say Mike Swenson hadn't learned well from his parents' mistakes.

Today, courtesy of Ginger Barnes, the bitter memories circled like sharks. Mike's dad in jeans and a Notre Dame sweatshirt. Dad, with his ironclad black and white rulebook. Dad, whose favorite endearment had been "loser."

And then there was his mother. "Pass your brother that last pork chop, honey, he's got a game tonight." Or, "Oh no, Mikey! Let Tad do that," when a monkey with a screwdriver could have assembled that bookcase.

The too-little, too-late change arrived wrapped in a blue cotton blanket—their first grandchild! Toys and clothes and gadgets accompanied every visit home. Photographs were snapped as if baby Jack were the reincarnation of Elvis. The phone lines hummed with questions about the kid's first burp, smile, rash, and coo. Dolores proclaimed that she missed Little Jackie terribly, "and you and your wife, too, of course."

Mike's dad congratulated him on "growing a pair."

Going underground had been complicated, but depriving his parents the way they'd deprived him proved to be enormously gratifying. Susan didn't know everything, of course; but she understood that disappearing had lifted a heavy weight. To reward her trust, he agreed to move back to her hometown…where she promptly acquired that stupid, stupid job, and he acquired the babysitter problem.

His heart had just about stopped when he heard Jack shout, "Daddy, daddy, daddy," from the park across the street. Miraculously, he distracted his co-worker with some BS about a reporter nailing the receptionist. Too close. *Dangerously* close. If Bob had turned his head and made the connection…

He dug an antacid out of his drawer. Chewed it with grim determination.

So the Barnes woman had followed him. Never mind how or why. The question fermenting in his gut was what to do about it.

Too soon to move again. Also, too suspicious. Susan's dad, her high school friends, that damn job…Mike's head began to throb.

Ten after twelve. He put his computer to sleep and headed for the stairs.

Emerging from the building, he breathed in the smell of warm asphalt and bread from the nearby bakery. The day was overcast, but dry. Two mothers had kids running around the park, but no Jack and no babysitter. Of course this wasn't one of Susan's workdays, so the Barnes woman could be anywhere.

As much as he tried to tell himself the odds of a babysitter bringing him down were infinitesimal, the reality was he didn't dare take a chance. Something had to be done.

He scanned the perimeter, bent down to peek inside parked cars, squinted to peer into the shade of a tree. No one hiding that he could see, yet the sensation of spying eyes burned into the back of his head until his vision blurred.

Each step striking a blow to his head, he detoured into the newspaper parking lot for the migraine medication he kept in the car. Swallowed the pill dry.

Relief was on its way in more ways than one.

He knew what he was going to do about Ginger Barnes.

Chapter 17

THE PAINT ON Chelsea's nose tickled, but her hands were unavailable, what with the roller in one and her cell phone in the other.

"My mother's coming Tuesday, July 1 to Sunday, July 6," Bobby confirmed over the phone.

Chelsea rubbed her nose against the shoulder of her t-shirt. "Hang on a second. I need to write that down."

"You'll remember."

"No, seriously, I won't," the visit freaked her that much. She traded the roller for the edging brush and wrote the dates on the newspaper under the paint can.

"How's the color?" Bobby asked when she returned.

"Awesome!" The cornflower blue looked vibrant, young, and fresh, although she worried that *Architectural Digest* might have been a better source of inspiration than Gin's dog-eared issues of *Country Life.*

"I'm sure it's beautiful," Bobby told her, and her face melted into an affectionate smile.

"I'll bring home dinner," he added, confirming that the honeymoon was still on.

Speculations about Marilyn Alcott followed Chelsea's paint brush around the doorframe onto the next wall. What did she know about her mother-in-law, really? That she wore tailored, coordinated clothes that made her look preppier than Chelsea's actual prep-school students. BUT! Did the woman play cards? Did she like movies? If so, which ones? Exactly what type of shopping did she like?

And how about music? To Chelsea, a person's musical taste said it all.

Her stomach growled, and her arm ached from rolling paint. Where the heck was her mother?

"Yoo hoo," the mother in question shouted up the two flights of stairs. "I'm eating with Cissie and Eric Zumstein. Back to work after that."

"Okay, Mom."

Chelsea covered the roller and brush, washed up, then scrounged up a lunch of pasta salad.

From her perch at the kitchen island, she could observe her mother's luncheon party without herself being seen. Seated on the back porch steps, Cissie faced the man, Eric Zumstein, who had sprawled on the ground beside baby Caroline's stroller. Gin, holding a paper plate and nibbling at a sandwich, appeared to be watching her companions with the intensity of a CIA agent.

Till death do us part; Chelsea's own marriage vows were so new that the words rang in her ears. Yet it was only now, seeing her mother from a different perspective, that she appreciated the huge boulder Gin was forced to circumvent.

Aunt Didi was right. It was time for Gin to put herself out there socially.

Perhaps Didi didn't realize her best friend was already doing that—her way.

Chapter 18

CISSIE HAD SPREAD a blue and white plaid football blanket at the bottom of her back steps. Eric sprawled across the part that covered grass and appeared to be comfortable, while I perched on the step beside Cissie and worried about my floppy paper plate falling off my lap.

The silence between the two strangers stretched on a beat too long, so I diffused it with some of my patented babble.

"My friend and I used to stuff our bologna sandwiches with pretzel sticks. Haven't seen pretzel sticks like that for ages." I'm sure I appeared vexed.

Baby Caroline dropped her stuffed giraffe from within her shaded stroller, and as Cissie bent to retrieve it, she remarked, "Potato chips might work."

I promised to give potato chips a try.

While the young mother flicked a strand of corn-silk blonde hair off her face, Eric Zumstein watched with fascination.

"Did you grow up around here?" he asked.

Smooth opening, and original, too. I bit into my sandwich to suppress a chuckle.

"Wisconsin."

Eric pretended to be appalled. "A Packers fan!"

"Not me." Cissie giggled. "I hate football. Did you play?"

"Nah. My high school didn't have a team."

"Where was that?"

"Philadelphia. And college..." He shrugged.

Our hostess took that in stride, but his non-answer raised my eyebrow.

"What did you study?" I inquired, the same time Cissie asked what he did for a living.

"I was a bank teller until last month. Having a helluva time finding anything else, so before I totally ran out of cash, I moved in with Gram."

When Cissie smiled, the sun shone a little brighter. "That's nice."

Eric erased the compliment with his hand. ""Expedient. She needs somebody to look after her, and I need a place to live."

"It's still nice."

I squirmed on the unforgiving step.

"She needs help because…?" I wondered aloud.

Eric immediately sat upright. "Because what?"

Because she's losing her grip?

"Because, um, because you're worried what she'll do?"

Eric was no longer the languid, I'm-on-vacation-from-my-grandmother lump on the grass he'd been the moment before. He lowered his eyebrows to say, "Why don't you tell me what you've seen?"

Now Cissie was staring and biting her lip.

I explained that I'd witnessed Maisie throwing a bag of clothes—and bricks—out of an upstairs window."

"Anything else?"

I consulted a cloud in the sky. "I've seen her carrying around a long rope, and a big knife."

A short laugh failed to hide Eric's discomfort. "My grandmother does read a lot of mysteries." I nodded as if giving that thought. "For entertainment, of course. They're not how-to books."

"Good!" I spread my hand across my heart. "Good to know she doesn't want to kill you.

"Although…She doesn't own a gun, does she?"

Eric's eyes widened. "Nooo…"

"Because I also heard a pop-pop-pop coming from your yard, and I smelled some really stinky smoke. I thought maybe it was from a gun."

A surprising expression took over Eric's face: infectious, eye-crinkling mirth. "Let me guess. You read a lot of mysteries, too."

I replied with a smile, but I was still waiting for an explanation.

Which was not lost on Mrs. Zumstein's very imposing grandson. "Would exploding eggs put your mind at ease?"

"Uh…"

"Gram was trying to make egg salad last week, but the water boiled away. Siss, boom, bang." He gestured wildly. "I tried to save the pot, but it was a goner."

His explanation actually made sense; I'd seen an abandoned pot among the mess at the Maisie's backdoor.

I placed the back of my hand to my forehead. "Phew. *That's* a relief. I was afraid my daughter was living next to Lizzie Borden."

Although the whole exchange had dismayed Cissie, she was once again beaming. "And I'm glad nobody's trying to kill you." Her hand casually patted Eric's knee, but there was nothing casual about his flinch.

"Oh, no," he demurred. "If anyone has a motive, it would be me."

The looks Cissie and I traded prompted Eric to explain. "I'm supposed to inherit the house."

"Nice," said Cissie, showing off her dimples.

"Not too soon," I said, finding my tact at last.

Already I'd seen and heard more than enough, so I gathered my paper trash and rose. "Better get back to work.

Thanks for the lunch, Cissie. Just the break I needed." *I'm so glad your husband didn't come home.*

The young woman stood to kiss me good-bye. "Thanks for everything, Mrs. B...er, Gin. I really appreciate it."

"No problem."

I eyed Eric as pointedly as I could, but he was too smitten to take the hint.

Chapter 19

AS CHELSEA'S mother rolled paint onto the last wall, Fideaux wandered in to give his owner The Look.

"My turn!" Chelsea exclaimed, eagerly setting down her paint brush. "Let's go, pal," she urged the dog, then hustled downstairs behind him.

When the duo reached the far right corner of the yard, Fideaux shot his hostess an almost audible, privacy-please glance until she turned away to survey her surroundings.

Now that she noticed, it was a lovely afternoon—blue sky, light breeze, a cabbage butterfly flitting around at random. The yard didn't offer much to write home about, but it was hers and Bobby's and she enjoyed an unaccustomed sense of ownership.

Nearby a male voice began to sing scales the way Chelsea had been taught to warm up her voice in college.

Unaware that she was in motion, she gravitated toward Mrs. Zumstein's detached garage. Situated halfway back from the house it sat snug up against the fence. Chelsea knew the small structure was stuffed with cast-off furniture and other junk; yet as she lowered herself cross-legged onto the grass, it became a theater.

"Oh boy, oh boy. Your pipes, your pipes are rusty..."

Eric Zumsteim. Had to be him.

A clearing of the throat and the song began in earnest. "Oh, Danny boy, the pipes, the pipes are calling/From glen to glen, and down the mountain side..."

Chelsea's jaw dropped. Even as a music major, she'd never experienced a live voice quite so heartbreaking. From a terribly expensive seat in the fiftieth row…maybe. Maybe.

"The summer's gone, and all the flowers are dying…"

No way could Chelsea exile herself from this. She crossed her fingers hoping her mother would understand.

"'Tis you, 'tis you must go and I must bide…"

She drew a deep jagged breath. Sure, the song was a guaranteed tear-jerker, but really! This guy was ripping her heart right out.

Next, "Ol' Man River," but like no other Chelsea had ever heard. Pulsing with pain, it filled her with empathy for the slave pulling the barge. Until Fideaux pushed between her arms and licked her face, she had been unaware that her cheeks were wet.

Then Eric launched into such an intimate "If I Loved You" from *Carousel* that she suddenly felt like a voyeur. Blushing to the roots of her hair, she rose from the grass and gently guided Fideaux toward the house. They slipped inside the backdoor with scarcely a click of the latch.

At the end of the day she held a trash bag open for her mother to stuff with soiled newspapers. "He's amazing," she repeated for the seventh time. "The guy should have an agent, a recording contract—fans!"

"Sounds like he already has one of those," Gin remarked.

Someone hammered on the front door.

Chelsea lowered the trash bag. "I'll go. My house, my ten-year-old fundraiser."

Yet when she arrived downstairs, she was shocked to recognize Eric Zumstein's profile through the window. For a second she feared he had come to scold her for listening to his rehearsal. But then he turned toward her, and she saw he was distressed about something much, much worse.

She opened the door.

"Is your mom still here?" he asked.

"Yes, upstairs."

"Can you please get her for me? I've got an ambulance coming for Gram."

***

"MOM!" CHELSEA SHOUTED up to me on the third floor. "Eric needs you. It's an emergency."

I threw down my paintbrush and ran down the stairs.

"Gram fell," Eric told me before I even reached the foyer.

When we were face to face, he explained. "She's pretty shook up, and she's confused, too. Thinks I'm her ex-husband, who's dead by the way, but she hated the guy and won't do anything she thinks he wants her to do, which includes going to the hospital. Could you please try to convince her...?"

"Lead the way."

"What's her first name," I whispered as Eric ushered me into the gray Victorian's front hall.

"Maisie," he said, "and thanks a million. I couldn't think of anything else to do."

"No problem."

Tucked under a blanket at the bottom of the stairs, Maisie Zumstein moaned with pain. In the distance we heard the strident approach of an ambulance.

"Maisie?" I said softly as I knelt beside the woman. "My name is Gin. I'm Chelsea's mother from next door. It seems that you had a fall."

Mrs. Zumstein met my eyes and nodded once. Tears trailed into the fuzzy hair that had fallen onto her face. I cleared her eyes and wiped her nose with the clean tissue I kept in my pocket.

"Don't make me go with him," the old woman begged. "Please don't make me go with him."

"I won't," I said, gently stroking her cheek. "But you should go to the hospital and get checked out. I can see that you're in pain."

The fright in the woman's eyes emphasized just how bad the pain really was.

"What should I do?" Eric asked from a discreet distance.

I asked him to grab her insurance cards and any meds she was taking. "Then why don't you follow us? Maybe ask Chelsea to follow you so I can get a ride back."

"You're going with Gram?"

"If they'll let me."

My stomach lurched to see the unnatural angle of Maisie's right arm as the emergency crew maneuvered her onto their gurney. I'm sure they were handling her as carefully as they could, but she cried out pitifully with each change of position.

Hovering as near as he dared, Eric shuffled and twitched and desperately tried to tell the EMTs about his grandmother's confusion. The two technicians were so focused on Maisie, I didn't think they were listening. But without taking his eyes off the patient the older of the two men responded.

"To be expected," he reassured her distraught relative. "She's had quite a shock."

When the time came to decide whether I should go or stay, the same EMT convinced me to stay. "If she gets upset, we'll tell her we're doctors, although the drugs should knock her out pretty quickly."

Chelsea and I stood helplessly on the sidewalk watching the ambulance roar down the street, siren blaring.

When it was out of sight, Chelsea put her arm across my shoulders. "Maybe you should move in with us," she said with mock earnesty. "My neighbors can't seem to manage without you."

I huffed out a little laugh, but that was all.

I was remembering Eric's unsolicited remark. "I'm supposed to inherit the house."

Chapter 20

"THAT'S BETTER," I told Jack the morning after Maisie Zumstein's fall.

We'd been pretending his toy horses lived on a ranch with a lake. Visiting their little plastic friends necessitated swimming from one side of the kitchen sink to the other, an activity that soaked not only the ranch but the entire countryside. And of course, Jack. I'd just changed him into dry shorts and another sleeveless t-shirt.

"Let's go out for ice cream," I declared. The TV weathermen claimed this would be the hottest day of the year, and for once I believed them.

Jack squealed and ran for the door.

"Hold up, Kiddo," I called after him. "I've gotta grab your diaper bag." And the car seat, and the shared house key. Mike wouldn't allow Susan to give me one of my own.

Threatening my waistline and Jack's lunch with ice cream was a no-brainer, but I also had a secret agenda.

"What a lovely surprise," Jack's grandfather responded to my invitation. "Meet you there in half an hour."

There was a local dairy farm that earned an A+ for marketing. Set a convenient two miles outside of Ludwig, it offered its own brand of ice cream and a selection of Pennsylvania Dutch specialties, such as Shoo-fly pie, Chow Chow, and fresh sticky buns. Displayed roadside were colorful flats of plants to tempt the local gardeners, and behind the shop were barns and pens of farm animals available for petting. In autumn there would be chrysanthemums and pumpkins, corn stalks and apple cider. I loved the place and knew Jack would, too.

"Ice cream first, cows second," I told the boy after I released him from his car seat. "Hey! Hold my hand in the parking lot." The encyclopedia of precautions required to keep a toddler safe, it had all come back.

"Hello, hello," George called from the entry to the ice cream parlor. "Jackie boy. I understand you're getting a treat for lunch. What flavor, eh? Chocolate? Vanilla?"

Jack bounced with excitement. "'nana choco chip."

George directed widened eyes at me. "Did you teach him that?"

"We talked about it a little in the car."

George regarded me with warmth. "And you know Jack loves bananas and chocolate. Looks like I recommended the right person for the job."

"Come, come." Jack tugged me toward the door.

"He's talking more, too," his grandfather observed.

"Jack's a smart kid. No holding him back."

I longed to interrogate George about the Swenson family dynamics, but I remembered my husband's effort to teach me finesse. "You can't just ask somebody if they're pregnant," Rip cautioned. "Ask if they have anything special going on this summer, something like that."

And so I worked on my wording while we waited for the freckled-faced college girl behind the tall counter to fill our order: a scoop of Banana Chocolate Chip in a cup for Jack, a caramel swirl sundae for me, and a double dip strawberry cone for George.

After paying, George dropped his change into the tip jar, and we went back outside to the half-dozen picnic benches shaded by four huge pin oaks. A welcome breeze blew the fragrance of eye-height cornstalks toward us from the adjacent field.

Since our ice cream was melting fast, I waited until we had that under control before I broached my delicate subject.

"I know the Swensons have moved around a lot," I opened, "so I got Jack a jigsaw puzzle of the United States to show him where he's been."

"You sure that isn't a little beyond our boy?"

"Never know until you try. Trouble is, I have no idea where all they've lived."

George took care of a strawberry drip before it landed on his knee. Then he gazed into the distance beyond the corn field.

"Mike and Susan were married in Minneapolis and adopted Jack soon after," he recalled. "Then it was Indiahoma, Oklahoma, briefly. Then Pollock, Louisiana; Montezuma, New York; Jacksonville, Florida, and here."

Except for the latter, dots on the map, I thought. Odd, remote dots on the map.

"Indiahoma, Pollock, Montezuma, Jacksonville and Norristown," I repeated to aid my memory. "Why those places, do you know?"

George's quick glance noted my skepticism. "Job opportunities, according to Susan. I told you I'm not that keen on my son-in-law. His employment record is one reason."

I helped Jack get a decent spoonful of ice cream, then I wrinkled my nose as if I were being playful. "You don't suppose he was into anything illegal?"

George failed to look as shocked as he should have. "It crossed my mind," he admitted. "But I decided if that were the case, they wouldn't have been able to adopt Jack."

"That's a relief then, isn't it?" I said, yet something still seemed off.

"I saw Mike come out of the newspaper building in Norristown the other day. Is that what he does, works for newspapers?"

Jack's grandfather shifted on the picnic-bench seat as if the question had made him uncomfortable.

"Susan doesn't always tell me what Mike's jobs are," he said. "I'm not sure she always knows."

"Sorry if I'm being too inquisitive." I gestured toward Jack to indicate my interest was on his behalf. Which, ultimately, it was.

George waved his head. "You're only asking the same things I've asked myself."

Returning to firmer ground, I inquired about the couple's wedding. "Was it nice?"

In spite of being flushed from the heat, I thought George paled. "I wasn't there."

"Oh." Oh, dear.

I shifted topics again. "I guess you're delighted they moved back here."

"Yes. Oh, yes," he agreed with a wistful smile.

So what if George Donald Elliot was an uptight insurance salesman; he was becoming a more complete person in my eyes, one who was understandably worried about his daughter's choice of a husband.

"Susan seems to love her new job," I observed.

"Oh, yes. I'm still surprised Mike came around, but I'm glad he did."

"I'm glad, too. Otherwise, I wouldn't be getting to know Jack."

"You like him, don't you?"

I glanced up at those unadorned golden-brown eyes and said, "I do," and to *my* surprise the corner of George's lips lifted.

The moment ended when I noticed a car driving by too slowly. The driver's face was shadowed, but he seemed to be scanning the property—including the picnic area under the pin oaks.

"Look!" I gestured toward the road just as the car sped up. "Is that Mike?"

"Could have been," George agreed. "He drives an old black Chevy."

Years of no intrigue, and now two situations that made the hairs on my arms bristle. If this was what opening myself up to the world was like, maybe I should stay home and learn how to knit.

***

THE GOOD NEWS was the inexpensive recording device Mike Swenson had placed on his home phone told him where Ginger Barnes would be at noon.

The bad news: his father-in-law was with her.

"Dammit!" He hammered the steering wheel with a sweaty fist. Waved his head with disbelief. Susan had sworn her father and the Barnes woman were not together. "No way," she'd told him. "Never happen."

And yet there they were.

Grill Susan again? To what purpose?

Mike's gut told him it was already too late.

Chapter 21

ERIC ZUMSTEIN MARCHED robotically from the parking garage into the lobby of Ludwig Memorial Hospital. With afternoon visiting hours about to begin, the needed elevator quickly filled with other family members eager to see their loved ones. Breathing in short, tense breaths, Eric stared ahead as if he was completely alone. Breaking free of the cluster at last, he focused on the checkered tiles of the third-floor hallway, glancing up only to check the passing room numbers.

Which Gram would it be today? The Maisie who greeted him as her one and only grandson, or the banshee who blamed him for her fall? Enough talk like that and people would take her seriously. Then what would he do?

The soft-blue single room possessed a framed pastel print of a flower garden and one sizeable window darkened by a thin-slatted Venetian blind. Nestled in crisp white linens, scowling in her sleep, its elderly occupant looked like a wrinkled, fuzzy troll.

Eric recalled one of the days he and his childhood playmate, James, had been parked at Gram's while their mothers worked. The two of them played Go Fish on the floor while Maisie watched "The Price is Right" on TV. Something Bob Barker said struck Maisie funny, and her raucous, staccato laugh scared the bejeezus out of James. Eric found his friend sobbing into his sleeve in the powder room under the staircase.

"What you blubbering about?" he demanded. Gram was the woman who baked peanut butter cookies and let him win at checkers. Whenever she laughed, he laughed even harder.

Now he finally identified with what James felt all those years ago—except with a significant difference. The threat Maisie posed was not in his imagination. It was in hers.

Convincing the old woman he loved her was crucial now, not only because of her wild claims about her fall. If she lived (as it appeared she would), and if he remained unemployed a while longer (as it appeared he would), some adjustments needed to be made. He could scarcely sleep, for one thing, and he itched from cat dander nearly all the time. Also, the house smelled like old skin, and he hated Gram's cooking.

Not much he could do about most of that, but some improvements could, and should, be made. The clutter, for instance. Easily half of Gram's possessions were overdue for the dumpster. Unfortunately, Eric feared suggesting even a modest cleanout might anger his grandmother so greatly she would toss him out.

Stalling, he sought out a nurse for an update. The white board under the wall clock identified the person on duty as "Shawna."

"She's with a patient," the woman at the central desk reported, "but I can ask her to come speak with you."

As an afterthought, Eric requested an extra blanket. Gram was always cold.

The woman waved to her left. "There's a warmer around the corner. Help yourself."

Two of the hospital's thin cotton sheets seemed just thick enough to kill the chill of the air-conditioning. Eric lay them across his grandmother as delicately as he could, but her eyes sprung open with alarm.

"Lonny," she almost screamed. "Get away from me!"

"It's Eric, Gram. Your grandson."

Maisie's gnarled fists gripped the edge of the flimsy covers. "Nurse!" she yelled. "Nurse! Get him out of here!"

"Lonny's gone," Eric assured her. Decades divorced, in fact. Five years dead. *You can stop now,* he wanted to shout. *Let it go. Move on.* But no. Maisie's hate had a life of its own.

"Liar," she snarled.

He tried a concerned smile. "How you feeling?"

The troll face narrowed into another scowl. "What do you care?"

"I care, Gram. Are you warm enough? Are you in pain?"

No reply.

When the silence began to stretch, Eric realized he would simply have to ask his question and roll with the consequences.

"About the house," he opened. "I'd like to get it ready for when you come home, but the first floor is already jam-packed. If you'll be sleeping there, and I'm already sleeping there…"

No way would he trade beds with her. If she couldn't do stairs, maybe her insurance would spring for a rental.

"How about getting rid of a few pieces of furniture? Maybe the burgundy sofa?" He had stumbled into it many a morning when he woke up on the adjacent sofa bed. "Whadaya say? Can I sell it, donate it? What do you think?"

"No!" Maisie gathered a wad of blanket to her chin. "Greedy pig," she added with hot, narrow eyes. "Greedy pig." She lifted her head as if she were aiming to spit.

"Now Gram," Eric responded reasonably. "Who are you talking to, me or Lonny? I moved in to help you, remember?"

"Nurse!" The old woman's voice lacked punch, and she hadn't pressed the call button. Maybe they wouldn't be interrupted just yet.

"I'm Eric," he tried again. "Your grandson. And I'm cleaning up the downstairs so you can get around easier when you come home. Help me out here, Gram. Tell me what you want to keep and what I can move out of the way."

"Leave my stuff alone. It's for my grandson, not you."

A young black woman in bright pink pants and a loose shirt printed with colorful flip flops tapped on the door jamb.

"Thief," Maisie barked at him. "I'll have you arrested. You hear?"

"Hi." The nurse greeted Eric as if she hadn't heard a thing. "I'm Shawna. You must be Maisie's grandson."

"Deadbeat!" Gram shouted. "Greedy bastard!"

"That's me," he said with an uncomfortable shrug. "Eric, the greedy bastard."

The nurse nodded. "When she's lucid, she asks for you."

"Thief! Rotten sonovabitch!"

"Let's step into the hall. You'd like an update, right?"

"Yes."

When they were safely out of Maisie's hearing, the nurse filled him in. "Aside from her arms and the hip, her blood pressure's up, and she's a bit dehydrated. Neither is unusual in the elderly. Easy fixes, both of them, although you should see that she drinks more fluids when she gets home."

Eric nodded. "I don't suppose she'll be doing stairs for a while, right?"

"Correct." The nurse tilted her head. "You know she'll need rehab first?"

"No, I did not know that. What do you mean rehab?"

"In a specialized facility. At her age hips take a long time to heal, and with her mental ups and downs she needs close supervision. Might be several weeks before she's ready to resume her everyday life. Even then, she may not have the mobility she had before."

Eric glanced through the open doorway. "She thinks I'm her ex-husband. What's with that?"

"She's in a weakened state. Traumatized, medicated. She's getting a neurological consult tomorrow. We should know more after that."

"What if her mind doesn't come back? What then?"

Folding her arms, the nurse stole a glance at her watch. "One day at a time," she answered. "No different from the rest of us."

She pivoted toward the next room and smiled her goodbye.

"Wrong!" he wanted to shout after her. Who else would be spending all day every day being mistaken for Gram's loathsome ex-husband?

For a second, a mere heartbeat, he imagined what life would be like without Maisie Zumstein in it.

The sky was blue.

***

ERIC DROVE home in a fog of emotions--regret, worry, confusion, loneliness, and more, but especially loneliness.

He considered calling Graham, his best friend back in Brigantine, New Jersey, but Graham was riding high on his internet marketing company success, and sharing his present woes would have made Eric feel pathetic in comparison.

There were others—Danny and Earl, Frogman, Patrick—but Eric had met them when he borrowed a bottle opener at an Eagles tailgate, and thereafter it was sports, sports, sports. He was pretty sure the guys had no idea he had attended a high school for the performing arts, and he certainly couldn't picture any of them sitting through a recital of his present predicament.

Yes, Gram's suburban neighborhood was the sort of place where those friends would settle down soon enough, but Eric was already there. The eclectic houses lined up like antiques on display, the park where little kids learned to climb and run and share, the sound of basketballs bouncing in a driveway at twilight, car doors slamming as the neighborhood hurried off to work in the morning. To Eric, this was already home.

He parked his old Pontiac next to the junky garage where he kept his voice in shape, although at this moment singing was the farthest thing from his mind. Right now he needed somebody to hear him, everything he could put into words, and everything else, too.

So compelling was his need that when he reached the front of Gram's old gray mare, he kept walking. Past Gram's property line, past the newlyweds place, straight up to the Voight's house two doors down.

Mounting the steps onto the porch, Eric hoped—make that *prayed*—that Cissie would be there, and that she would let him in.

Chapter 22

ALTHOUGH SUSAN was punctual for a change, by the time I grocery shopped, threw in some laundry, and fixed dinner for Fideaux and me it was evening before I got to do what I was so eager to do—put on pajamas and sit down at Rip's old computer with a glass of merlot.

"Indiahoma," I recited, typing in the Oklahoma location Susan and Mike had chosen soon after their marriage.

It had been a while since I'd indulged in a little harmless snooping, and I caught myself hunched forward in pounce position, snitching quick sips of wine, and grinning like a Cheshire cat. Even if all I learned was that Mike Swenson liked to move his family around, so what? It was my time to waste as I pleased.

Turns out that Indiahoma is situated between Oklahoma City and Wichita Falls slightly off Route 44. The old want ads I found were for truck drivers, medical professionals and military trainers, but especially medical professionals. Opportunities to work from home were also plentiful but usually required an investment of money up front. The town's population was evenly divided between men and women, the total a mere 380 souls with an average of 38.64 years. Many were Native Americans or Hispanics with a small assortment of assimilated Europeans.

What I really needed was access to the archives of the local paper, *The Lawton Constitution*, and that, too, required money up front. Sixty cents for a one-day account.

"I think I can afford that," I informed Fideaux, but the dog had fallen asleep.

Knowing the year the Swensons married would have helped, but pressing George for more detail would have made him suspicious. I went with my best guess—three years ago—and spent an hour delving into ancient Oklahoma news. If I encountered so much as a hint of criminal activity by anyone named Swenson, I planned to phone the appropriate police department and hope they could put my worries to rest.

Nothing turned up. The only fishy part of the family's brief residence in Indiahoma was Indiahoma itself. From the look of it, people were moving out, not in. Plus it just plain seemed like an odd choice.

Stop Two: Pollock, Louisiana, easily remembered because of the artist famous for splashing paint on large canvases. A good-looking guy starred in the movie. What was his name? Another search for another night.

Pollock, the town, appeared to be part of Grant Parish in the Alexandria, Louisiana, metro area, population about 368 in 2003, named for a guy who owned a lumber mill. Employment opportunities leaned toward store managers and the same come-on, work-at-home jobs offered in Indiahoma. I chalked that up to the site I was consulting rather than a trend. They also needed a U.S. Army Chaplain.

Potential pay dirt! Fifteen miles north of Alexandria in the middle of the Kisatchie National Forest, a United States Penitentiary needed correctional officers ASAP. A couple more mouse clicks informed me of an adjacent minimum security prison for slightly less scary male offenders. The convenient "inmate locater" assured me that no Swensons resided there either now or three years back.

Stop Three: Montezuma, New York, a pinprick on the map west of Syracuse just south of Lake Ontario. Influenced by a trip to Mexico back in the early 1800s, New York doctor Peter Clark named his soggy estate Montezuma. Neither the extraction of salt, a necessary industry if not an especially lucrative one, nor the Erie Canal bothered Peter's marshland much, but the Cayuga-Seneca Barge Canal built in 1910 lowered the water a drastic ten feet, and humans have been trying to repair that shortsighted error ever since. Dikes, for instance, and the reintroduction of nesting eagles. Nothing, however, prevented lots of carp from infesting the pools when Cayuga Lake overflowed, and unfortunately these "nuisance fish" bred and ate and pooped themselves into trouble with the species in charge.

The reported population of 1,431 were mostly Caucasian, so the Swensons would not have attracted attention in that respect. Although the average income for males was higher than at the family's previous stops, over fifteen percent of Montezuma's residents still lived below the poverty level.

More and more I wondered what jobs Mike might list on his resume. And why such obscure places to ply his trade, whatever it was?

Next came Jacksonville, Florida, and since that move actually made sense, I allowed myself to go to bed. My concentration was gone anyway.

Comfortably nestled down, my fingers twined in Fideaux's kinky fur, my last waking thoughts were about Susan. My personal reservations about her aside, I had difficulty imagining her staying with a violent man. Nor could I imagine the wife of a violent man taking a job over her husband's objections.

Anyhow, it seemed to me that most criminals (the ones in the annex, not the high security prison) were primarily after money, and none of the tiny hamlets I'd researched offered much temptation in that regard.

They were, however, excellent places to hide.

Chapter 23

RONALD VOIGHT'S life was turning to shit. On top of the Cissie thing, the site manager had ragged on him about his daily report. "You call this quality control? What the hell have you been doing all day?" High and mighty sonovabitch. Probably never missed a payment. Probably never had anything worse than a hangnail in his whole friggin' life. What if *his* wife let another man into the house in the middle of the day? See if the short fat fuck could concentrate with that going on in his head.

He'd picked up his neighbor's message ten after twelve and called right back. Had to be about Cissie, because he'd asked Harry to keep an eye on her.

"Hey, man," his old drinking buddy opened. "Sorry to bother you, but..."

At first it sounded like Harry messing with him. Unemployed, bored, and soused most of the time, there was an even chance he was jerking his chain. But no. He put his wife on, and Evelyn swore on their kids' heads that her husband was sober. So it was with disbelief and anger sizzling through his veins that Ronald told Harry to say it all again.

"I got a good view from the front room, as you know," Harry reminded him, "your front door and mine maybe forty feet away, fifty tops. So it's lunchtime and I was taking turns watchin' TV and lookin' out the window, and there he is. Big guy. Big! Two thirty, maybe fifty, that big. Seems to be stayin' with that old lady. Anyhow, he parks in her drive and walks down the sidewalk plain as you please. Then he knocks on your door like maybe he's a long-lost friend or somethin'."

"Yeah?"

"Yeah," Harry told him. "Then the door opens and in he goes."

"How long?"

"Hour. Maybe hour and ten minutes."

"See anything else?"

"Naw. The door was closed."

"Thanks, man. I owe you."

"No problem."

Except there was a problem, a huge problem. He wanted to kick down a tree. The world was a blur. His head was so swollen with fury all he could hear was the buzz of his own blood.

Never in a million years would he have figured Cissie for a cheater. Didn't he keep a roof over her head and food on the table? Damn right, he did. And the way she oohed and ahhed over that kid, you'd think she had everything she could possibly want.

He, on the other hand, had plenty to complain about. One glance and Cissie used to jump. Breakfast, beer, sex, *whatever*, she fell all over herself trying to please him. No more. Those days were gone.

Ronald locked up the company pickup and strode to his car.

His usual pub started out quiet but soon filled with noisy men, construction workers softening the edges before they went home to deal with their own women and kids. Any other night he would have been one of the back-slappers, in the thick of the crowd trading jokes and complaints.

Tonight he kept to himself at the short end of the bar and ordered his bourbon neat. The bartender, a skinny guy with the ridiculous notion of growing a beard, eyed him from a safe distance. Only a matter of time before he got flagged.

We'll see about that. The bourbon condensed his anger, toughened him, tightened his fists until he felt capable of taking on a heavyweight champ.

He raised his hand to signal the bartender.

The next thing he knew he was being man-handled into a cab.

***

CHELSEA HAD PUT the finishing touches on the guest room then cleaned all afternoon. Now she longed for a shower and a guilty half-hour in front of the TV before Bobby came home. But first she needed to unload the dishwasher, make the first impression complete. The *voila* factor, as she thought of it.

The open window over the kitchen sink offered a slight breeze laden with humidity. Probably a thunderstorm overnight. Her mother-in-law might have a messy trip in the morning.

Glancing toward the street as she peeked past the trees, Chelsea noticed Eric Zumstein depositing a loaded box on the sidewalk beside their trash can. Because of the township's limits, he'd asked permission to add some of his overflow to theirs.

"Getting ready for when Gram comes home, whenever that will be." He'd looked so forlorn Chelsea had been tempted to hug him.

Just as he set down a second huge box, a taxi pulled to the curb and disgorged Ronald Voight.

Loose limbed and stumbling, Cissie's husband shouted at Eric. "You! Get away from my house."

Chelsea rushed to her front screen door but hid behind the door jamb where she could both see and hear.

"You sonovabitch! Stay away from my wife."

"We talked," Eric responded with remarkable calm. "You should try it sometime. Your wife's a smart woman..."

"Why you..."

Eric stood solid as a fireplug while Voight jabbed his collarbone, moved within inches of his face.

"You. Were. With. My. Wife."

"We talked," Eric repeated. "Nothing happened."

Ronald's first punch landed soft, but his second connected hard.

Eric waved his head. Rubbed his upper arm. Muttered, "Neanderthal."

"What'd you call me?"

Another swing. Another feint. Then it began full force, a free-for-all of kicks and jabs and obscenities.

With longer arms and an extra thirty pounds, Eric easily held off his drunken attacker, but he soon tired of the inconvenience. Intercepting Ronald's wrist, he forced Voight's arm up behind his back.

"Get sober," he warned. "Then get yourself a brain." He shoved his attacker flat on the sidewalk then turned back toward his grandmother's.

Voight regained his feet. Wiped his bleeding palms on his jeans. Followed Eric's retreat with hate in his eyes.

Then, just as Chelsea feared, Ronald broke into a run and tackled Eric from behind. Darting for the cordless phone in the living room, she could hear the men wrestling no-holds-barred on her front lawn. She was telling the 9-1-1 operator her address as she yanked open the screen door.

"Stop!" she hollered as she ran down the steps. "I called the police. Stop stop stop..."

She was still holding her trembling fist to her lips when the police arrived. A clumsy scuffle ensued, but the officers loaded him into the patrol car without too much difficulty.

When the door finally shut on Ronald with a resounding "chunk," Chelsea allowed herself to check on Cissie's whereabouts.

She was just in time to see a curtain drop back into place in one of the Voight's upstairs windows, the only indication that Cissie even knew the fight had happened.

The patrol car left in a cloud of exhaust, and Chelsea shepherded Eric into her kitchen to address the damages.

Scrapes and bruises mostly. For a man who hadn't played football, he'd defended himself awfully well.

Although…

"You better watch your back," she warned as she angled a band-aid across his swollen knuckles.

"You, too."

Chelsea dropped his hand and stared.

She hadn't thought of that.

Chapter 24

SINCE I DIDN'T babysit on Thursdays and had stayed up following the Swensons' around on the Internet the night before, naturally my bleating cell phone woke me at 7 AM.

"Uh, hello?" I mumbled.

My son's laughter hit me like a shot of adrenaline.

"Garry! How come you're up so early?"

"Going sailing," which figured. He was calling from Cape Cod. "Anyway, you're usually awake. Hot date last night?

"You wish."

"Everybody wishes that except you."

"Next," I warned. "To what do I owe this pleasure?"

"I need something, of course."

"I'm listening."

"White shirts. About four or five."

"Interesting. And why do we need these shirts?"

"Because I got a job."

I panicked just a little. "Up there? What will you be doing?"

"Waiting tables. Again."

No complaints there. Chelsea had worked as a server, too, and it had forced her to become efficient. The downside was I'd be deprived of my son for another two and a half months.

"It's a really cool restaurant on the water, so the tips should be awesome. At least a couple hundred a week. Maybe more."

I forced my voice to remain level. "Where will you live?"

Garry blew a hefty sigh into the phone. "Mule, the brother who invited me up here, has a friend with a pool house that doesn't get used. They sort of hooked me up."

So my son had some new friends who liked him enough to want him to stick around all summer, and he liked them well enough to want to stay. Also, the money was nothing to sniff at.

Garry further argued that his former yardwork customers had surely made other arrangements by now and that mowing lawns didn't offer much of a social life.

"These are good guys?" I pressed. "No drugs, drinking binges, no screwing around?"

Garry laughed. "You know me better than that."

I assured him I did. He was as upstanding a young man as a mother could hope for, a fine testament to the influence of his father. "It's your fraternity brothers I don't know."

"They're good guys," my son affirmed, "especially Mule, short for Meuller, by the way. And you'll like this—the pool house belongs to a judge."

Relaxing, I stretched my legs so far that Fideaux groaned in protest. "So do I send the shirts, or what?"

"Yeah, I guess. I have to start work Friday."

Trying not to sound crushed, I urged him to tell me about his vacation. Garry related a couple of comical stories that were clean enough to share with his mother, then I delivered abbreviated versions of my babysitting job and Chelsea's visit from her mother-in-law.

I signed off with the acceptably unsentimental, "I love you, kid," but in the silence after we hung up, it hit me.

My baby had moved out.

***

MOVEMENT WAS my antidote for loss. Any activity would suffice, but, due to the summer heat and my new job, Fideaux and I had acquired the habit of exercising early. I dug my rubber gardening shoes out of the basket by the backdoor and grabbed Fideaux's short green leash off the hook.

"Want to go for a walk in the park?" I shouted. "Walk" and "park" were the only words he would process, but whole sentences sounded less demented if a neighbor happened to hear.

And I hoped someone did overhear. Since I'd been widowed, the idea of my neighbors seeing me, hearing me, knowing when I was home and when I was not, comforted me, even if the comfort was probably a delusion.

"Up, up!" I told Fideaux when we got to the car, and he eagerly hopped in.

Parked at the side of the most popular entrance to the woods were a plain black sedan I didn't recognize, a large professional-looking van, and an SUV belonging to a woman with a Sheltie named Hobo. Hobo herded Fideaux and nipped, so I kept my timid darling leashed so I could help fend off the pest.

We didn't see another soul for half a mile.

"Proves how big this place is," I commented, remembering the time a little girl had run from her parents in a huff, only to get lost in the woods. Police had enlisted the help of regulars like me to find her, but my only proof that she got rescued (and it was no proof at all) was the absence of police activity the next day.

To brighten my outlook, I focused on the beauty of nature as I tromped the root-riddled downhill path. The cool air smelled of rain-soaked mulch and ozone, and a glance upward through the trees told me the clouds were thickening again. Only when I reached the long flat stretch beside the creek was I able to pick up my pace.

Which was when I caught a glimpse of white about thirty yards ahead. Probably because Garry had just requested white shirts, I thought it was a man's elbow disappearing behind the trunk of an ancient sycamore. Yet it just as easily could have been a flash of sun through the trees. Fideaux hadn't reacted, though, and he never missed a chance to check a stranger's pocket for dog treats.

After the third broad wooden bridge crisscrossing the creek, a wall of ancient boxwood hedge nearly closed off the path. Once a studied part of the original landowner's estate, the park volunteers had hacked an opening that allowed the many walkers to continue.

On a sunnier day I might have imagined myself as Alice stepping through the looking glass, but today's growing gloom conspired to make me jittery.

Still, here I was. Where else was I to go?

I grasped Fideaux's leash tightly and pressed ahead.

Twenty yards later, the man I'd nicknamed The Hunter marched toward me with his index finger pointed at my nose. His pale face and receding blonde curls were damp from exertion, his expression angry.

"*You* are *single*," he scolded.

"What?"

My reaction prompted a smile. "You let me think you're married, but you're not."

I blinked and gulped. "How did you find that out?"

The smile widened. "I asked around," he reported with an arm wave that encompassed the entire park. "You shouldn't mislead people like that. It isn't nice."

Too shaken to be anything but blunt, I stated, "I'm not interested in dating." What if he planned to follow me home?

What if he was a murderer or a rapist? Most of all, how was I going to handle this new development?

Charlie's owner, I finally remembered the dog's name, raised his eyebrows. "We'll see," he said. "We'll see." Then he called to his German Shorthaired and marched past Fideaux and me with what I hoped was make-believe righteous indignation.

"I was being *tactful*," I muttered quietly enough not to be heard. I hadn't been pursued like that in a couple of decades, and a small but rambunctious part of me wanted to break out the champagne.

"Guess I'm not totally over the hill," I bragged to my dog. "Whaddya think of that?"

Then I remembered about shaving my legs, changing outfits seven times before a date, makeup, and *flirting* with silly getting-to-know-you questions like, "Did you grow up around here?"

Yuk, I decided.

Double yuk.

"Let's go home," I informed my pet.

Fideaux performed an about-face and bolted for the hole in the hedge.

Chapter 25

WHEN CHELSEA arrived at the train station, the macadam was still giving off wisps of moisture from last night's deluge. After slipping into the second-to-last parking spot, she stepped out into the damp sunlight. With rainwater leeching into her sneakers she made her way to the nearest kiosk and inserted her credit card with trembling fingers. Marilyn Alcott would be here in ten minutes or less.

Since meeting a train was nothing Chelsea did on a regular basis, she had nothing to do but wait on the platform with her purse dangling in front of her. Nearby, a woman urged her toddler to say the word "locomotive," again and again. An elderly gentleman huddled on the metal bench inside the glass windbreak reading the *Daily News*. Pacing to Chelsea's right, another man tried to convince somebody to buy imported truck beds over the phone. Chelsea pondered how she was going to entertain her new mother-in-law.

The silver commuter train arrived at last. With clatters and thumps and the squeak of brakes it stopped four feet in front of Chelsea's face, enveloping her in its hot-metal stink. Two men in light summer suits exited like rabbits released from a trap. Next came two teenage boys with skateboards, which they rode down the wheelchair ramp to the parking lot. A pair of women chatting about arthritis, and finally Marilyn Alcott.

Red faced from struggling with her suitcase, her eyebrows peaked with dismay. She was a petite, strawberry blonde with wiry-thin arms and apple cheeks. Despite the rigors of travel, her grooming remained perfect.

"Mrs. A," Chelsea called up the steps. "Let me help you."

The conductor stepped forward to grasp his passenger's delicate hand, so Chelsea squeezed by to wrestle with the suitcase, an ordinary black thing that seemed to weigh a ton.

After the train moved on, Marilyn raised her arms for a hug. "Darling!" she trilled.

"Welcome," Chelsea croaked into the woman's ear. They had met so infrequently before—a couple of holidays, a dinner and a show in New York for her father-in-law's fiftieth birthday, a weekend visit to plan the rehearsal dinner, and, most recently, the wedding. Kissing seemed presumptuous.

Marilyn presumed. She bussed Chelsea loudly on the cheek with her hand behind her head and hugged her a second time. "Sweetheart," she said. "It's so good to see you."

Chelsea felt her shoulders inch down from their fortress position. "You, too," she agreed, as she realized it was actually true.

Following the teenagers' example, they used the wheelchair ramp down to the car, which made pulling the suitcase a breeze.

"We're going out to dinner with my mom tonight," Chelsea reported. Let somebody else cook, had been the original thought. Include someone from Marilyn's age group was the second.

"Sounds lovely."

The suitcase snuggly stuffed into the trunk and her houseguest snuggly belted in, Chelsea turned the ignition key.

The radio blasted *"Don't Touch My Hat"* into their faces.

"Whoa, there." Chelsea swiftly lowered the volume. "Sorry." She'd been thinking of her own mother and had subconsciously put on some of Gin's music.

"That's Lyle Lovett, isn't it?" Marilyn exclaimed. "Love him. Never could see him with Julia Roberts, though. How did you get hooked on him?"

"Mom put me onto him years ago."

"Oh, darling. We're going to get along, aren't we?"

Did that mean Marilyn and Gin, or her and me?

Chelsea answered yes.

***

THE CLOVERS, as the restaurant was called, was a known commodity—white linen, a broad range of food choices, a no-rush policy, and prices the young couple could afford now and then. They held hands and beamed at each other like Cheshire cats.

For the occasion Gin had donned a silk, moss-green sweater so bland you were drawn to her mischievous eyes by default. In contrast, Marilyn Alcott wore an impeccable peach-colored dress and gold flats. White purse, discreet pearl earrings.

As the two older women scooted to the middle of their semi-circular booth, something about Gin's demeanor put Chelsea on edge. When her mother ordered a certain cabernet before checking the price, she felt certain hell was about to freeze over.

Then it happened. Gin asked if Marilyn liked to cook. It was her mother's favorite trick question, the one she used to take measure of another woman no matter what the answer.

Chelsea couldn't help it; she groaned out loud.

Marilyn's reply was remarkably prompt. "I cook to eat."

Gin laughed and tapped a knuckle against Mrs. Alcott's bicep. "Good one," she said. Then she scouted around for their server, probably longing for the bread basket.

Marilyn appeared to have detected something, but she wasn't sure what. She simply stared blankly into the middle distance.

"My mother doesn't cook," Chelsea tried to explain. "She makes food."

"Ah," Marilyn responded, but a silence ensued.

Everyone made a show of consulting their menu. Orders were placed, and the bread arrived.

Gin's cheeks were now brighter than her eyes, and Chelsea worried that her mother might require a ride home.

"What are your interests?" Gin inquired next, and Chelsea allowed herself to breathe.

Feet finally back on firm ground, Marilyn confided, "Gardening is my passion. Did you know you can plant bulbs with an electric drill?"

Gin reared back with delight; a power tool had been mentioned. "No kidding. What happens if you hit a rock?"

Marilyn drew in her lips to suppress a giggle. "You'll break the bit, which I must say, makes my husband very, very mad."

"Over a drill bit?"

"Oh, yes. Lawrence loves his tools. You should see our garage." She leaned Pisa style toward her son's mother-in-law. "Sometimes I call him 'Lug Wrench,' or just plain 'Lug.' He hates it, of course, but it lets out some of the wind, you know?"

The food came, and they all applied themselves.

A small skirmish occurred when the check arrived—Gin and Marilyn both risking their water goblets to grab for it. Bobby was younger and quicker, however, so the mothers exchanged tight-lipped grins and put their hands back on their laps.

In short order they were settled into the backseat of Bobby's car. Pierced ears were being discussed, which Gin labeled, "Barbaric," although hers were pierced. "Like contact lenses," Marilyn agreed, but she used them, too.

Back in the newlywed's driveway, they hugged their farewells. Chelsea reached for Bobby's hand and got a warm squeeze in return.

Then a sound no one ever wanted to hear ruined the soft summer twilight.

Gin was the first to move. She ran along the hedge between the kids' house and the Voights until she could see into the next backyard.

Abruptly stopping beside her mother, Chelsea recognized the figure in a white shirt and light slacks sitting on the Voight's kitchen steps.

"Cissie, is that you?" Gin whispered through the hedge.

Cissie startled at her name and gasped back a sob.

Gin pushed through a gap in the hedge with Chelsea right behind.

With a gentle hand, Gin lifted Cissie's chin for a good look at her face. A swollen red area on her cheek would shortly become black and blue, and the way the young mother clutched her stomach made it horribly clear that her cheek was not her only injury.

"Ronald?" Gin guessed.

Cissie scrambled back against her kitchen door. "It was my fault," she claimed. "He didn't mean to do it."

"Anything broken? Do you need a hospital?"

"No! No hospital."

"What about Caroline? Is she okay?"

An emphatic nod.

Gin glanced up at the house.

"Your husband still here?"

"Ronnie'll be right back. He just needed to calm down."

"Get Caroline and come with me."

"No! Really, Ms. B. I'm fine. You can go home. I don't need any help."

Trying to diffuse her mother's intensity, Chelsea tapped Gin's arm.

"We'll go," Chelsea assured Cissie, "but if you need help anytime, you come running, okay? Bobby and I are right here. Grab Caroline and come get us. Promise?"

Cissie released a ragged breath. "Sure. Sure, thanks."

"Come on, Mom," Chelsea tugged at her mother. "Bobby and I can take it from here."

Gin was close to tears herself, but she got it. Cissie couldn't be forced to do anything she didn't want to do. It was also possible outside interference would make the situation worse.

"You should get out," the mother in Gin implored anyway. "Go somewhere safe."

Hiding her face behind one hand, Cissie waved them away with the other.

Chapter 26

WORRYING ABOUT Cissie's injuries kept me awake past 2 A.M. I found it impossible to understand how a man justified hurting anyone, let alone the woman he claimed to love. What kind of perverted worldview permitted him to cross that line?

I'd been lucky enough to marry a kind and caring man, who, fortunately, stayed that way. Initially, Ronald must have been kind and caring, too; but since his sort of behavior required a woman he could overpower, control, and ultimately abuse, he must have deliberately selected a woman with insecurities he knew he could exploit.

And what about his daughter? Would Caroline someday become his victim, too? The very thought made my skin burn.

To comfort myself I fingered Fideaux's fur as his ribcage gently rose and fell with sleep. Sadly, I knew much of his devotion was rooted in gratitude, for it was quite likely he had also been abused. While I will never understand, nor forgive such cruelty, one thought provided me with a thin hope. Fideaux had found me. With luck Cissie would find a rescuer, too.

Perhaps she already had someone in mind.

***

I AWOKE the next morning with Fideaux's head on my foot and pins and needles in my toes. Through the open window I could smell dewy grass and sunshine.

New day. New perspective. Life was made up of contradictions, I reminded myself. Highs and lows, flowers and children, sickness and Ronald Voights. Since Cissie had rejected my best advice, which she had every right to do, my only option was to back off and mind my own business. But, damn, it was hard.

At least it was Friday, and I would be busy with Jack. He scarcely fussed anymore when Susan left for work, and my efforts to expose him to new things appeared to be paying off. I especially loved how his eyes sparkled with mischief when he was trying to make me laugh.

Crossing the Dannehower Bridge toward Norristown, I noticed a wide stripe of jet stream spanning the soft blue sky. It had begun to separate into fluffy white clumps, but no one born after Wilbur and Orville Wright would have mistaken it for a natural cloud. For sure, George Washington would have been intrigued.

"Jet exhaust," I imagined myself educating Washington's ghost. "From above it looks black."

A tilted white eyebrow.

"From an airplane."

Blank stare.

Oh, right. "We have machines now that carry people across the sky like birds. Well, not exactly like birds. The wings are metal and they don't flap."

Machines?

Out of deference, I allowed George the last word.

Now I was ready for a day with a toddler.

***

I TOOK Jack to Produce Junction. Originally a regular grocery store, the gutted building was now open space where customers shunted past help-yourself tables of colorful, prepackaged vegetables. At the wooden checkout tables two vendors swiftly grabbed the rest of what you wanted from bins stacked behind them. Because of the bulk quantities, I hadn't shopped here for a couple of years; but I figured potatoes and onions would keep until I could use them up.

"And leeks," I decided at the last second. I would make potato/leek soup. "And cilantro," for salsa I added, as the man behind me began to fidget.

Jack held my hand, but he was itching to run. "No, no. Stay here," I begged. With a second's head start he would be lost among the many shoppers.

"Zat?" he asked, pointing.

"Red peppers," I answered as I collected my change.

"Zat?" This time rutabagas.

"Rutas," he repeated. And so it went all the way out to the car—me carrying my heavy box of vegetables and naming everything at Jack's eye level.

What I'd really come for was a flat of white impatiens, but that involved another line outside. When that purchase was settled into my trunk, I freed one of the three-inch seedlings from its plastic compartment to show Jack the roots.

"See these little white things? When it rains, they drink the water and send it up the stem to the leaves and flowers. It's like you drinking with a straw."

Jack grinned. "Again," he said, so I obliged.

"Again," he repeated, and so I did. This was the good stuff of our day. That and the cuddling while I read him his favorite picture books—over and over.

After a lunch of noodles and peas, I began to carry him upstairs for his nap.

"Oo-ett," he said as he played with a strand of my hair.

"What's that kiddo?" I'd been daydreaming, a sign that I could use a nap, too.

"Oo-ett."

"You're wet? Wow! What a smart boy you are." Throughout the diaper change I reused the word and praised his burgeoning brilliance. I could scarcely wait to tell Susan about the breakthrough.

Yet when Jack's mother arrived home, twenty minutes late, she wanted to share doctor's-office gossip. Jack woke during a juicy tale about somebody's date gone wrong, so Susan gestured for me to follow her upstairs. A hasty reunion hug and kiss as she finished the story, then the young mother finally fell silent while she changed her son.

"Tell Mom what you told me," I urged the boy.

He met my eye but held his tongue.

"Wet," I whispered.

A flash of recognition. "Oo-ett" he responded with a giggle.

No reaction from Mom.

"Did you hear that?" I hinted.

"Hear what?"

"Jack said 'wet.' He knows when he needs a new diaper." Now that it had been pointed out, surely Susan would recognize how precocious her child was. Surely she would praise him to the sky and back.

"Um hum. Mike is talking about moving again. Do you know anything about that?"

Thrown by the abrupt change of subject, I stepped back and folded my arms across my chest. "About your moving? Why would I know anything?"

"Oh, I don't know. Mike's been acting strange, and sometimes he asks about you."

"Asks what about me?"

"If we talk…what we say when we talk…"

"But we don't. This is more than we've said to each other in two weeks."

"Yeah, I know. Sometimes Mike's a little paranoid."

I thought of the day George and I saw a black Chevy like Mike's driving slowly past the dairy farm and rubbed down the hair on my arms. Only yesterday I got spooked by a sleeve disappearing behind a tree. When I'd indulged my curiosity about the Swenson's various moves, all I'd learned was that they had made peculiar, *potentially* suspicious, choices. Yet if Mike really was running from something and viewed me as a threat...

But why on earth would he think that?

Jack securely on her hip, Susan fixed me with a loaded expression.

"You're not like, interested in him, are you?"

"Romantically?" I nearly choked on my laugh. The age difference alone made the thought laughable. "Is that what you mean?"

Susan smiled, but without mirth. "I didn't think so. I mean, you look really young, but…but what do I know? Stranger things have happened."

I placed a reassuring hand on the woman's shoulder. "Let's sit down and think this through."

With Jack in his high chair occupied with a handful of Cheerios, Susan and I settled across from each other at the kitchen table.

"Mike isn't the least bit interested in me, nor I in him," I stated, because it had to be said. I might have added, 'perish the thought.' "But lately I've felt that someone's been watching me. Does that sound like Mike to you?"

Susan rolled the corner of a paper napkin between her fingers. "Maybe. Like I said, he can be a little paranoid."

The way my pulse raced, I had to work to sound unaffected. "Really?"

"Yeah, that's why we've moved so much."

"Because he's paranoid?"

Susan nodded, and auburn hair bounced against her cheeks. "His ex-wife is a real bitch. He's terrified she'll find us."

"How come?"

"Money, of course. He owes her a bunch, and we just don't have it." Susan glanced around the room. "Hard to imagine living any tighter than this."

Yet many people do, I might have said, but I desperately needed to leave this woman's house before I snatched up her delightful, thoroughly unappreciated son and took him home with me.

"Oh, look at the time," I remarked to grease my exit.

I gave Jack's cheek a loving pat and reached for my purse.

Chapter 27

FIVE DAYS LATER I returned to my daughter's house, this time for a casual dinner to celebrate Marilyn Alcott's birthday. I'd assembled my good-enough-for company meat loaf at home, a glorified cheeseburger, really—and presently it was in Chelsea's oven along with roasted red potatoes and a something involving corn.

When all the guests had drinks, Bobby lifted his glass, "To my mother, may she have a happy year and many more."

Marilyn's hazel eyes beamed at her son while Didi, Will, Eric from next door, and I all clinked glasses and murmured birthday sentiments. Chelsea emerged from the kitchen in time to kiss her mother-in-law and add her best wishes. "Just a couple more minutes on the meat loaf," she said as she sat down.

Eric turned toward me. "You left a note and some books for Gram the other day," he said. "That was nice of you."

Never happy living with an ill opinion of anyone, I'd visited the hospital with some paperbacks for Maisie hoping to erase my doubts about her grandson. With luck she would be lucid enough to share more details about her fall. For instance, where had Eric been when it happened—upstairs or down?

Since my agenda hadn't been completely altruistic, I swallowed a dose of guilt along with a sip of water.

"Unfortunately, your grandmother was so sound asleep I didn't get to talk with her. How's she doing?"

"Not as good as yesterday." With his lowered brow and stiff demeanor, I couldn't quite gauge how Eric felt about that.

I murmured my regret about Maisie's downturn.

"Yeah, me too."

Again, that little pin prick of distrust, which I forcefully brushed aside. This was a birthday party, after all, not an inquisition.

After dinner was served, I took the opportunity to ask Chelsea if she'd spoken to Cissie since the incident.

"I've seen her in the yard with Caroline a couple times," my daughter replied. "She didn't seem hurt or anything, just unhappy. I can't imagine what it must be like to be her." She made a point of addressing the latter to Will, the psychologist in our midst.

Compassionate guy that he is, he took the bait. "What's your neighbor's problem exactly?"

Chelsea explained, then redirected her sympathy toward Eric. "He knows," she said with a gesture. "Ronald attacked him, too."

Will's professional countenance invited honesty, and Eric responded without hesitation. He waved his head in wonder as he said that Ronald had accused him of "being with" his wife.

"But we just talked," Eric insisted with obvious frustration. "I know it was stupid to go there. I wish to heaven I hadn't, but my grandmother was in trouble, and..."

"...and you didn't want to be alone." Marilyn patted his hand. "We believe you, darling. Don't blame yourself. Bullies like Ronald Voight will use any excuse to throw their weight around, isn't that right, Will?"

"Yes, actually, it is," Will agreed. "Abusers are a rather interesting sort. Not at all what most people think." He peered at the bit of potato on the end of his fork then popped it into his mouth.

I leaned toward him from across the table. "*Why* aren't abusers like most people think?"

Will sent a glance around the group. "First, I'll tell you what an abuser is not," he began with practiced timing. "He is not mentally or emotionally ill. He was not necessarily abused as a child, although he may have learned from such an experience. Alcohol doesn't trigger the violence..."

Marilyn's mouth dropped open. "Then what does?"

Will contemplated the valance over a window before meeting her eyes. "He simply gives himself permission to lose control."

"But...?"

"Why?" Will asked back, gesturing with his fork. "Because the man is entitled, don't you know? His desires are the only ones that count, and everything he does is calculated to make the world deliver the privileged life he is absolutely positive he deserves."

"That's why he hurts his *spouse*?"

Will nodded so hard his sandy hair flopped onto the top of his glasses. "Since he's so superior in every way, anything that goes wrong for him must be her fault. If he loses his job, it was because her nagging distracted him. The car runs out of gas? She didn't fill the tank. He'll even twist her complaints around until he convinces her she's to blame for them, too."

We all expressed outrage until Will held up his hand. "And," he continued, "although the problem has nothing to do with his feelings, the woman will go overboard trying to make him feel better about himself. She'll walk on tiptoe to keep from setting him off and worry obsessively about what he'll do next. It's diabolical, really. The abuser has her fixated on meeting his needs first and foremost. Then to obscure his egocentric motives, he deliberately keeps her off-balance."

"Like how?

"Large ways and small. He demands dinner promptly at five. Then when it's ready, he goes out to mow the grass. He demands sex whenever he wants; but if she initiates it, he's not interested. Most likely he's cheating, but God forbid if she does. The woman literally can't win."

I had to whisper over the lump in my throat. "Why does Cissie stay?"

Will's voice softened. "Because her husband's dramatic apologies and spates of good behavior are extremely convincing. And before you ask, yes, it's all been calculated to avoid any inconvenience to him.

"He also goes to great lengths to make sure everybody else sees him as a swell guy. That way, if his wife ever works up the nerve to tell the world what a bastard he is, nobody will believe her."

To put the topic to rest, Chelsea stood. "Anybody want their dinner reheated?"

The microwave was employed, the main course consumed. Much to everyone's relief, the conversation traveled far from the minefield of domestic abuse to topics like interest rates and how to grow tomatoes.

Bobby stuck multi-colored candles—one for each guest rather than for each of his mother's years—into the ice cream cake. Then lights were lowered and "Happy Birthday" sung as he carried it to the table.

Chelsea and I had been looking forward to everyone else's amazement when they heard Eric Zumstein's voice; but he simply folded his hands and listened.

What's that all about? my daughter's raised eyebrows inquired, and I answered with a shrug.

When the singing stopped, Bobby instructed everyone to make a wish then choose a candle by putting their ring around it, if they were wearing one. "The person whose candle burns out last gets his or her wish," he explained.

Marilyn blew out the seven flickering flames, and one by one the orange wicks blackened. Eric's ringless one held out longest, and the rest of us clapped and cheered over his impending good luck.

"Don't tell the wish," Marilyn warned, "or it won't come true."

Eric flicked her an uncomfortable glance. In spite of Will's cautionary "cheating" remark, the young man's desires were transparent. I believed him when he said his friendship with Cissie Voight had been platonic—so far; but how long that would last depended on willpower and prudence, two very unreliable virtues when hormones are involved.

I tagged Will to help clear the dishes; and when we were alone in the kitchen, I returned to the topic that preyed on my mind.

"Is it typical for an abuser to withhold sex?" I wondered. Cissie's confidential complaint seemed to be at odds with the behavior he'd described earlier.

The psychologist nodded as he set a plate in the dishwasher. "I'm afraid so," he said. "It's another power play, another way to assert control and insure the woman's best efforts."

With my lips in a grim line, I covered a bowl with plastic wrap. "It started when Cissie was pregnant."

Will nodded again. "Some men have a mental ideal, and when the woman's body no longer matches up..."

I closed the refrigerator hard. "How do you convince a woman to break away?"

The psychologist rinsed another dish. "It's easier when the relationship is new," he said. "After a while the pattern becomes so entrenched it's almost as if she's a prisoner."

"So much for Women's Lib."

"Preaching to the choir," Will murmured sadly. "Reasonable men got it. The others prefer not to."

Chapter 28

AFTER BIDDING FAREWELL to her mother-in-law at the train station Tuesday morning, Chelsea found herself in her front vestibule wondering which way to turn. She considered tackling the wedding presents in the second bedroom, but they could wait awhile. Instead she poured herself some iced tea, picked up the newspaper, and strolled into the backyard.

Parking herself on the uncomfortable plastic chair the previous owners left behind, Chelsea stretched out her long legs.

Summer! No classes. No meetings. A giddy laugh burst out of her, and she glanced around self-consciously before realizing she was quite alone. Cissie had been hiding for days, and Eric seemed to be either cleaning out his grandmother's house or visiting her in the hospital.

Extracting the Arts and Entertainment section of the paper made Chelsea think of Eric's amazing rendition of *Ol' Man River*. What fun it would have been had he sung at Marilyn's birthday party! Everybody would have gushed and fussed. Brimming with confidence, Eric would vigorously pursue his dream. Success would flow like champagne...

Instead, he hadn't sung one note, and Chelsea was dying to know why.

"If you want an answer—ask the question," she preached to her students. But who was there to ask? If Eric refused to sing so much as "Happy Birthday," giving him the third-degree about it would be the worst thing she could do. Also, if she confessed that she'd heard him rehearse, the garage concerts might end.

The Internet offered a much safer start. Cheered by the prospect, Chelsea propelled herself off the unforgiving chair and returned to the house. Settling down with her laptop on the dining room table, she signed on and typed "Philadelphia schools for the performing arts" in the Search box. After the picnic lunch at Cissie's house, Chelsea's mother mentioned that Eric's high school hadn't offered football, which made sense. He had probably attended a specialty school designed to nurture his talent. Not Chelsea's own route since she'd chosen her music later than most, but Eric's gift would have been obvious well before high school.

One hundred eighty possibilities popped onto the screen. Many were dance studios or limited to instrumental instruction. Two schools admitted only elementary-age students. The revered Settlement School had a long and successful history, but the nuts-and-bolts academics were left to others. Because of its promising name, Chelsea clicked on The CEG Performing Arts Academy, but it focused on acting, ballet and belly dancing. A second site of the same name offered dance and modeling instruction. She was aware of The Curtis Institute of Music's astounding reputation, but theirs was a college level program. That left only the Philadelphia High School for Creative and Performing Arts on Broad Street.

A couple clicks later she had the name of the two people responsible for the Vocal Music Department. Time to talk to a real person. With only a little trepidation, Chelsea punched the school's number into her cell phone.

The receptionist forwarded her call to the first name listed; but no one answered. It was late June after all. Her second try also went to voice mail.

Not feeling very hopeful, she requested her third choice, and a counselor named Ms. G. Benge picked up on the second ring. After introducing herself, Chelsea asked if the woman remembered a student named Eric Zumstein.

A sigh carried across the line. "Sad case," the counselor bemoaned. "One of my failures, I'm sorry to say. What's your interest in him, if I may ask?"

Good question. Chelsea chose to keep it brief. "I've heard him sing."

"Then you're one of the rare lucky ones," Ms. Benge replied. "A voice to make the angels weep, but the worst stage fright I've ever encountered."

Chelsea's pulse pounded in her throat. "You worked with him? Personally, I mean?"

"Yes, for all the good it did. I'm a guidance counselor, not a therapist, but I've had a number of stage-fright cases over the years."

"What did you do?"

"Same as I did for the others. Positive reinforcement."

"Did it help?"

"Didn't do a damn thing. Eric was usually able to sing in a chorus, but solo performances were his personal hell. And his is a solo voice if ever there was one.

"I also had him stand alone on stage with no one in the theater and let him have all the time he needed to calm down. He stood there over an hour, but it just didn't happen. Tragic. I have no idea what he's doing now. Do you?"

Chelsea related what she knew, that he'd been working at a bank in New Jersey, but when he lost that job he'd come to live with his grandmother, "next door to me."

"How is it that you heard him sing?"

"He was vocalizing in his grandmother's garage, and I happened to be out back."

"So now you're making him your own little project. Are you single by any chance?"

"Married. I'm a music teacher."

"Oh, well then. You're in."

Chelsea overlooked the hint of sarcasm. "What do you mean?"

A wry chuckle. "Eric only sang solo for his vocal coach…in a soundproof rehearsal booth."

Ms. Benge had washed her hands of her "worst failure," once; and apparently she was ready to do so again.

Chelsea thanked her for her candor and promised to let her know if anything came of her own efforts.

A grunt and a dial tone ended the conversation.

Chapter 29

ERIC STOOD WHEN the lanky man in green scrubs stepped into the waiting room and called his name. When they were close enough to approximate privacy, his grandmother's surgeon clasped his hands behind his back and tilted toward him.

"Ms. Zumstein's operation went fairly well," he stated with a wan smile.

"Fairly?"

"I'm sure you realize she was fragile already. Her recovery depends on how much fight she has left."

Eric blinked openmouthed long past the time for a question, so the surgeon nodded, pivoted on his heel, and disappeared back through wide mechanical doors.

A hand grabbed Eric's forearm. Dr. Quinn, Maisie's attending physician. He stood a mere five-foot seven to Eric's towering six-foot three; a slight hundred and sixty pounds to Eric's two-twenty. Instinctively, he overcompensated with post-straight posture and a lifted chin. Today his eyebrows crouched together in troubled thought.

"Come with me."

Without waiting, the doctor led Eric around a corner into a bland sitting room with seating for two to eight people. He closed the door, gestured at the chair a knee's length from his own, then propped his elbow on a small round table of fake blond wood.

"What do you know about your grandmother's accident? *Latest* accident," he quickly corrected. His voice conveyed grave concern, his expression, too.

Eric rubbed a hand over his head. He'd been drinking coffee like an addict since his grandmother's fall earlier in the day, and now he could scarcely hold still.

"What do you mean, what do I know?" Eric touched his jacket pocket to check on his inhaler.

"How do you think she managed to remove her IV, lower the bedrail, and fall out of bed *with her right arm in a cast and a broken left wrist?*"

Eric's head felt gripped by a vice. "You can't think I had something to do with that."

Quinn lifted his chin higher and pursed his lips.

Eric glared at his accuser askance. "My grandmother is a determined woman. If she wants to do something, she does it."

The doctor sucked his cheek. "So you may say, Mr. Zumstein, but I'm not inclined to believe you."

"Believe whatever you want. I wasn't even there."

"Really, Mr. Zumstein? The nurses saw you."

Eric sighed with impatience. "I was down getting coffee."

Quinn folded his arms across his chest, a TV District Attorney doubting a witness.

Eric breathed. Folded his own arms. Addressed the ceiling. "You know how you tell a kid not to touch an electrical outlet, and the next minute you catch him poking it with a fork? That's Maisie Zumstein. That's Gram." Eric shrugged and spread his hands.

Quinn looked aghast. "Are you saying she pulled out the tube because she knew she wasn't supposed to?"

"No," Eric drew out the word. "I'm saying she's wicked clever and more stubborn than a Billy goat."

"If she wanted anything, her call button was right there."

"Not in her nature to ask for help."

"Enough of this nonsense," Quinn shouted into Eric's face. "She was sedated, Mr. Zumstein. Sedated!"

"Are you sure about that?"

The doctor forced himself to settle down. "Of course I'm sure. She was experiencing anxiety, so the nurse requested a sedative."

Eric's eyebrows rose. "Only half-true. She was throwing one of her crazy, delusional hissy fits, and I requested the sedative myself. She couldn't have gotten it, though, *because she'd have been asleep.*"

"My point exactly."

"She was not sedated."

"It was noted on her chart."

"And the nurses do whatever you order them to do the instant you ask?"

"Yes!"

A tap on the door, and one of the uber-obedient nurses stuck in her head.

"Ready for you, doctor."

Quinn rose to go. "I am not satisfied with this discussion, Mr. Zumstein."

Eric reached into his pocket for his inhaler, "Not my problem," he told the closing door.

***

AT TWO FOURTEEN the next morning Eric was awakened by a call from the hospital. His grandother had suffered a stroke moments before. "She's gone, Mr. Zumstein. We did everything we could…"

Suddenly the cold room, indeed the whole house felt hollow, sucked dry of life. Emotions too numerous to name invaded Eric's   being the way an army overwhelms a stronghold. He realized he'd smashed his fist on the adjacent end table only when the objects on it crashed to the floor. Tossing his phone aside, he sat with bare feet on hardwood littered with ceramic bits and lightbulb shards.

He covered his face and whispered, "Sorry, Gram," into the void. "I'm so, so sorry."

Chapter 30

"YOU SOUND WEIRD," my daughter remarked when I answered her call the following morning.

"Exercise," I confessed. I'd been doing some actress's muscle-toning routine on the living room floor. "What's up?"

"Bad news," Chelsea warned. "Mrs. Zumstein died early yesterday."

"Oh my! What happened?"

"She fell out of her hospital bed and broke her hip. She survived that surgery, but they think a blood clot probably broke loose and caused a fatal stroke."

I murmured something appropriate.

"Yeah," Chelsea agreed. "Rotten luck, but it gets worse. Cissie says the doctor was extremely rude to Eric. Practically accused him of causing the fall. He was so rattled he phoned Cissie at her house."

"At least he didn't go over," I thought out loud. "How is she? Do you know?"

"Okay for now." Chelsea explained that when she'd noticed Cissie bringing in her trash can, she had scurried out for hers just to check on her next-door neighbor. "That's when she told me about Eric's call."

"What had the doctor said to Eric?"

"That he doesn't believe Mrs. Z could have removed her IV by herself, not with a broken left wrist and her whole right arm in a cast. She'd been sedated, too.

"I don't know, Mom. It does sound suspicious, but Eric said he wasn't anywhere near the room when it happened."

I appreciated that my sensitive daughter preferred not to think ill of her private singing project, but I also remembered how frightened Maisie had been of her grandson after her original fall. So frightened she refused to let Eric accompany her to the hospital. At the time Maisie had believed Eric was her ex-husband, so I'd assumed her fear was part of her delusion.

The doctor's suspicions prompted me to have second thoughts. Mistaking a face was common among the elderly; failing to recognize physical danger was not. So it wasn't impossible for Maisie to be wrong about who Eric was but perfectly correct about the threat he posed.

Although the second accident may not have directly caused Maisie's death, any fall at her age certainly held that potential—as anyone who'd seen how fragile she was would have known.

"The funeral is eleven on Saturday. You want to go?" Chelsea inquired.

We agreed to go together, but not for the same reasons. While I applauded my daughter for wanting to nurture Eric's talent, if he'd had anything to do with his grandmother's death, I wouldn't hesitate to orchestrate his downfall. Would I hate for that to happen? Certainly. But for Maisie's sake—and my daughter's long-term safety—I would.

Still, my internal conflict disturbed me the rest of the day. I hammered down an exposed deck nail so hard that the impact bruised my hand. I scowled at the ground all the way through the park and back; and when the government census guy came knocking again, I slammed the door in his face.

*＊＊＊

BIG SURPRISE. What men did when they were gone all day wasn't the magic act Susan Swenson had been led to believe. The paycheck in her purse proved she could do it, too; and the revelation made her feel as if a larger, stronger woman had taken possession of her body.

She also saw her husband with fresh eyes. Watching him across the table as they ate a late supper, he seemed ordinary, like just another guy eating and drinking and talking about himself. Where was the powerhouse she'd married back in Minneapolis? When had he become a thin-haired, pasty-faced Clark Kent?

At long last the monologue about the fluctuating economy and how it irked Mike personally sputtered to an end, and Susan had her opening.

"Where were you this afternoon? I called your office, but you weren't there." She'd been obsessing over how to deliver those lines ever since she'd spoken to the newspaper's receptionist.

Shock registered on her husband's face in slow motion.

"It was the third time in three days, Mike. Where have you been?"

"I'm not listening to this shit." He grabbed his empty drink glass.

Susan dogged him to the kitchen. Leaned loosely against the doorjamb. "I'm just curious," she stated in what might have passed for a reasonable tone. "Why can't you answer me?"

Mike gave her one of his long-suffering sighs.

"I was working, Susan."

"Doing stuff for the paper." Even to her she sounded snotty; and, just that fast, super-Susan deserted her.

"Yes. Doing stuff for the paper. I *work* for the paper, remember?"

She was sniveling already, but now that she'd started, she needed to finish.

"The receptionist said Ernie's been all over you for taking too much personal time. Is there somebody else, Mike? Do I need a lawyer? Tell me. I have a right to know."

"Oh, for God's sake, Susan. I've been looking out for you and Jackie. Same as always."

"But Cathy said..." The receptionist. The person who set this train wreck in motion.

"Cathy has a big mouth." Mike moved as if to leave the room, but he couldn't get past. "Do you mind?"

This close he felt like the hot stove Susan's mother had warned her never to touch.

Voice thin as glass, she asked if they needed to move again.

Mike put his hands around her arms. The chill of his drink glass made her shiver. "Don't I always take care of you and Jackie? Eh? Don't I?" The look in his eye resembled pity. "Don't I?"

Susan averted her face, tucked her chin tight against her shoulder, gave him the required, "Yes."

Victorious, Mike wheeled away.

Then he turned back, forced himself to speak calmly into the hair that covered her ear. "I'll kiss Ernie's ass for a week or two, put in a little overtime, and be back on track. Don't worry, Suze. Okay? That's an order."

He clamped her in a tight, if not loving, embrace.

She was ready to let go first; but, as it was, she had to wait for him.

***

CISSIE VOIGHT ACHED to her bones. The baby had a summer cold, maybe even an ear ache, and until moments ago cried every time she was put down. It was midnight now, and little Caroline had finally—finally—succumbed to her own fatigue.

Cissie lay rigidly alongside her husband, facing the window to pretend she was alone. Unencumbered by concern, Ronald had begun to snore seconds after his head hit the pillow. He hated air-conditioning, or air-conditioning bills, he never said which, so the bedroom window was raised five inches—too narrow for Cissie to float through and fly away, open enough to suggest another world beyond these walls.

Ever since the first awful meltdown, each time Ronald came home had become a cruel game of Russian roulette. Some days Cissie got a husband who wanted nothing more than for her to be his wife. But too often a controlling tyrant came through the door, a man it took heaven and earth to please. And when he wasn't pleased, the blows landed on body parts where a bruise wouldn't show.

She wished she didn't know how he portrayed her to their friends, but the information arrived second, and sometimes third hand—gossip disguised as concern, nosiness masquerading as advice. "Are you okay? Ronald says you've been acting strange ever since the baby, like maybe you need help." "What a catch that Ronnie is! You better look out or some young babe will steal him. Maybe even me." Ha ha ha.

Merely speaking to Eric on the phone was a terrible risk, but their conversations had become Cissie's link to the outside world. Without the comfort of Eric's voice she feared she would lose her mind.

And now he was in trouble. She sensed it in the hushed way he told her about his grandmother's death. He sounded frightened, maybe even guilty. But of what? She refused to pursue the thought. He was her lifeline, and now she would be his.

Silent tears made cool trails across her cheeks. Life could be simple, she thought, if it weren't so complicated. In spite of everything, she still cared for her husband, still hoped and prayed he would become the husband and father he promised to be.

That he would hurt his child seemed unfathomable, but even the slightest chance he might raise his hand to Caroline became Cissie's most compelling reason to stay. Men were being granted sole custody left and right these days, especially if the woman was a screw-up. And, as Ron was so fond of reminding her, she was a mess.

Chapter 31

MAISIE ZUMSTEIN'S funeral took place in the smallest parlor of the Huff and Metcalf Funeral Home on East Lansing Street. A smattering of folding chairs projected an underwhelming attendance while soft, completely forgettable, recorded music underpinned the few awkward conversations going on. Long shadows from the heavily draped windows contrasted with three harsh strips of sun and so dulled the three sprays of flowers displayed behind the deceased's urn, that you couldn't help thinking how quickly the flowers would suffer Maisie's fate. The trail of worn carpet looping from the right-hand doorway, around the front, and back saddened me further, while the stuffy smell of clothing too long in the closet tempted me to hold my breath.

Chelsea and I waited our turn with the immediate family behind two elderly women in flowered hats and low-heeled shoes. They agreed that their Uber driver was "very nice" but he needed a haircut.

While the old sweethearts jabbered, I observed Eric in between greetings. Hands comfortably linked together below relaxed arms, he rocked gently forward and back on shiny, perhaps new, brown dress shoes. His pale gray summer suit was appropriately somber, and his downcast eyes suggested peace or contentment. What jarred me was his smile. Eric Zumstein was very pleased about something.

He could be thinking anything, of course, but the hint of self-satisfaction in his grin turned my imagination down a dark path. Was he secretly thrilled to have his grandmother gone? Was it possible Maisie's doctor was right, that Eric had calculated this outcome and set it in motion?

The grieving grandson returned before the next person leaned forward to speak, but my discomfort remained. To dispel it I shifted my attention to Eric's brother, Wynn, and their parents, Ida and Abe.

Abe caused one of the flowered-hats to stare and pout in response to her condolence, which piqued my curiosity about him.

"How do you know my mother?" he challenged when we faced each other and forward progress stalled. A flabbier version of his sons with a smoker's gray complexion, he seemed oddly inhospitable for the circumstances, so I was slow to reply.

Eric freed himself from a teary kisser just in time. "Ms. Barnes helped get Gram to the hospital when she fell, Dad. Her daughter, Chelsea, lives next door."

Abe's scrutiny seemed to intensify.

"You should thank her, Dad," Eric suggested, but that got a nod so curt I stepped aside to let the next person in.

Chelsea finished grasping Ida's small hands with both of hers. "Sorry about your mother-in-law," she murmured. Casting her own critical glance toward Abe, she pecked Eric on the cheek, shook Eric's brother's hand, then joined me in my search for a seat.

There were still plenty to be had; the gathering numbered a paltry fifteen including the undertaker. We chose the third row on the left, and behind us two septuagenarians gossiped about Maisie loudly enough for us to hear.

"That's the grandson been living with her," said Number One.

"Not married, then?" observed Number Two.

"Out of work."

"So that's how she got him to take care of her."

"Nah, remember that rabbit-fur jacket Lonny bought her? Made him sneeze something awful, but she wore that thing till it was almost bald as me."

"I'm not following you."

"I'm just sayin' Maisie had a way, that's all. Whatever she wanted always came out sounding like somebody else's idea."

The discussion ended with the appearance of a pseudo-clergyman in a black blazer who launched into a lengthy, and surprisingly cheery, homily that could have been about anyone. Then at last the mourners were permitted to stand and talk among themselves.

My daughter and I bolted for our car.

"Why did we do that?" Chelsea asked as she belted herself in.

"Good question." I refrained from speeding out of the parking lot sheerly by willpower. "Lunch?"

"You bet."

We chose an upscale eatery with leather booths and an inventive menu. I ordered iced tea and an Asian salad festooned with green shrimp. Chopped cashews and wasabi peas added texture. In my opinion it needed a side of sandwich to qualify as lunch.

"What was it with Abe?" Chelsea wondered aloud. "Did he think we were crashers or something?"

Since I was busy with a cashew, I shrugged.

"As if anybody would crash a funeral. What for? They didn't even offer water, and hey—it's eighty-eight degrees out there."

Watching Chelsea wrestle some Romaine into her mouth, it occurred to me that my daughter hadn't attended many funerals. Perhaps only her father's, and I wished to high heaven she hadn't had to attend that.

I said, "Maybe Abe picked up my vibes."

Chelsea stopped what she was doing. "What were you thinking?"

"Tough man to have for a father."

Chelsea nodded hard, poked her salad, then kept poking until something stuck on her fork. "So do you feel even sorrier for Eric now, or is it just me?"

While I weighted my words, I waved our waiter over and begged for rolls.

I concluded that I should not share my misgivings about Eric with Chelsea. Not yet anyhow. She liked the man, and suggesting he might be less than admirable before I had proof would not be well received. With luck, I might never have to say anything.

However, I did agree that I felt sorry for him. "I can't imagine an old grouch like Abe being thrilled with a son who sings."

Chelsea slapped the table so hard I jumped. "I have a plan. You want to hear it?"

"Sure."

"Eric can sing in a chorus, but solo—forgetaboutit."

"Okay…?"

Eyes glittering, my daughter pushed her salad aside and leaned in. "Stage fright is a phobia, right? And since psychologists help people get over phobias, I thought maybe you could ask Uncle Will to help. What do you think?"

What I thought was that most professionals hate being hit up for "freebies" from their friends, and why not? It's presumptuous and rude. On the other hand, Will had *willingly* offered his expertise regarding Ronald Voight, so I only waffled a little.

"Maybe he could steer Eric toward the right kind of therapy."

"Yes!" Chelsea exclaimed. "So you'll ask him?"

Aloud, I answered, "Of course."

Chapter 32

MIKE SWENSON checked his watch for the twentieth time.

Eleven forty-three; worth the risk. He glanced briefly around the newsroom before making his way downstairs like a man on a mission.

"Picking up a prescription for the kid," he lied to the receptionist, tapping her desktop on his way past.

"Yeah, sure," Cathy muttered without glancing up.

So focused on what had happened this morning, he was through the door and outside before her indifference registered. Was it only yesterday, she'd freaked out his wife with innuendoes about another woman? Thank goodness Susan had still seemed contrite this morning.

If only Ginger Barnes could be handled so easily.

"Mister Swenson," she had greeted him first thing this morning; and, like the ring of a hammer, the name had reverberated in his head ever since. *Mis-ter Swenson. Mister Swen-son. Mister Swenson*, until he was positive the use of his new surname meant far more than hello.

Anxious to do something about the babysitter's mounting threat, he shoved his car into gear and joined the town's weekday traffic. Chewing his lip and squinting into the sun, he drove without aim.

Ginger Barnes must be neutralized. He knew that. But how and when? Confronting her before he was 100% certain she knew something risked arming her with information she could take straight to the police.

Which meant all she had so far was unfounded suspicion, otherwise the police would have shown up already. He braked hard for a stop sign.

Swenson, Swenson, Swenson! It had to mean something. His stomach churned with indecision. Perhaps if he monitored the woman's behavior every chance he got, an answer would somehow become obvious.

He eased forward with care. Realized he was almost at his own street. Idling at its mouth, he saw no sign of the babysitter's red Acura. She must have taken Jack somewhere for lunch.

Three possibilities came to mind, all within a block of each other.

He turned his Chevy around and drove.

***

"WHAT'S DIDI UP to today?" I asked Will after we settled Jack into his high chair at Kentucky Fried Chicken. Hello kisses had been exchanged and food collected.

"I got chickin," Jack loudly announced to the nearest newcomers.

"She's teaching dance to inner-city kids this afternoon," Will answered. This was obviously a day he worked at home, because he wore a green golf shirt and a fancy sports watch coveted by runners. "Before that, I don't know."

Jack twisted in his high chair to address two teenagers. "I GOT CHICKIN!"

Will's lips twitched. "While it is always lovely to see you, Ginger dear," he tilted his head toward the boy, "perhaps you should tell me why we're here while you can."

"Thank you," I replied as a blush infused my cheeks. Toddlers' meltdowns did occur without warning; and Will and I had never met for lunch before. Me wanting to pick his brain was a given.

Yet how was I to start?

Behind his designer glasses Will's hazel eyes patiently waited.

I occupied Jack with his water cup before getting straight to the point. "Eric, Chelsea's neighbor from the birthday party, happens to be a phenomenal singer. I've heard him, and he really is amazing. Frank Sinatra, Josh Groban caliber."

"Can't get any better."

"Right. So Chelsea, The Music Teacher, wants to help him become rich and famous. Live the dream, and all that."

"Does she?"

"Does she what?"

"Want to live the dream?"

"No," I answered, although the question gave me pause. "At least I don't think so. She likes teaching little kids and conducting." Plus she was married now and, I hoped, wanted kids of her own—eventually. Not that being rich and famous would prevent that...

I waved my hand to erase the line of thought. "Mainly, I think she's excited about discovering an exceptional talent."

Will tried to hide his bemused smile by saying, "But...?"

"Fries!" Jack hollered, so I gave him a handful of mine.

"Yes, but," I continued, "Eric gets stage fright. Paralyzing stage fright. In a chorus where he can't be singled out he's fine. Alone with his vocal coach, fine. On a stage by himself—can't do it."

"I noticed he opted out of 'Happy Birthday' the other night, but I figured he was one of the many of us who can't sing."

"Well, he can—and he can't. What can be done about it, Will? Anything?"

"Oh, yes.   Cognitive behavioral therapy, exposure therapy, virtual therapy, hypnosis."

"All that?"

"Hi! I got chickin!"

"Yes, Jack. You got chicken all over you. Ketchup, too." I dipped a napkin in my water and began to clean the boy's face and hands. Over my shoulder, I asked, "Which one do you think would work for Eric?"

Will said he would have to interview Eric to figure that out. "Can you set it up?"

I dropped the napkin along with my jaw. "I wasn't expecting you to personally..."

Will pushed his paper plates aside. "Sounds like a worthy cause, and an interesting one."

"Do you have time?"

"For a friend of yours, of course."

Was Eric a friend of mine? Until proven otherwise, yes. "Thanks," I told my best friend's husband, wondering yet again whether I should have come clean with my worries regarding Eric's innocence.

Sobered by the thought, I fell silent as Will and I made our way to the parking lot. I was carrying Jack and my shoulder bag, so Will walked me to my Acura and helped me settle the toddler in.

As I turned back to say good-bye, I saw a man in a parked car overlooking the restaurant duck down out of sight.

My immediate impression was of Mike Swenson, possibly because the car looked very much like the one Mike drove. Considering this wasn't the first time I had gotten this impression, the coincidence gave me chills.

"What's wrong?" Will asked.

I watched as the car pulled back, revealing only the passenger's side. As it shot forward and disappeared, I remembered that Jack would hear my answer. "Nothing," I told Will. "Just looked like someone I know."

"Someone you don't like," Will observed.

I chuckled. "Very astute, Doctor. The guy I thought it was does give me the creeps, but he would be at work now, so no worries."

"We're not all monsters, you know."

"Of course not," I concurred. Then I thanked him for being such a good guy and gave him a proper hug.

Chapter 33

NO NERVOUS GIGGLES today. Susan tossed her shoulder bag onto a chair then slumped down after it. I couldn't be sure, but I thought her eyes gleamed with tears.

"Tough day?" I guessed.

"Tough week."

I shut off the rerun of *Law and Order* I'd been watching. "Jack ought to sleep another hour. How about some coffee?" universal code for *"Would you like to talk?"* If I was getting too personal, Susan could decline or steer the conversation elsewhere.

She agreed with a weak flip of her hand.

From the kitchen I watched my employer's shoulders shake with silent sobs.

"Cream and sugar?" I called to her, as if nothing was the matter.

"No, thanks."

When the coffee was done, I set a mug in front of her. Eyes still red from weeping, Susan took a sip then set it aside.

"What's wrong?" I prompted gently.

"Mike, of course."

"Trouble at work?" If so, it had nothing to do with me. At least I hoped not.

"Sort of. He's been missing a lot of time."

"Oh?"

"Yeah. I called the paper three times when he wasn't there. Somebody told me his boss has been complaining."

"About him missing work?"

An unhappy nod. "At first I thought it was another woman. It still might be. But maybe not. I just don't know."

"It certainly isn't me," I asserted, at least not in *that* way.

Susan managed a brief laugh. "I guess I knew that," she admitted. "I was just so upset. So confused."

"No worries. It was sort of a flattering mistake. Crazy, but flattering."

Susan smiled to herself then met my gaze. "You're okay, aren't you? I mean, you're really a good person."

"I try."

Her sigh was almost a yawn. "I sensed that right away. It was just that Mike..."

"I thought that about you, too." I had, but there were other issues I questioned now, like why she agreed to adopt a child if she didn't especially like kids.

I suggested that we start at the beginning. "Maybe we can figure this thing out."

"Oh, I don't know..."

"Humor me." I set my own coffee next to Jack's puzzle of the United States, the one I'd bought to trace the family's moves. "Mike didn't want you to take the job, right?"

"Right."

"Help me understand why."

Susan shrugged as she glanced around the sparse living room. "He just likes me home with Jack."

"Is he really that old-fashioned?"

"Yes," she finally answered, drawing out the word as if there were more.

"But...?"

Her eyelids lowered. "Mike's ex-wife, 'The Bitch.'" She enclosed the latter in finger quotes. "Mike doesn't want her to find us, so he doesn't trust anybody he doesn't know."

"Like me."

When Susan began to protest, I lifted my hand to interrupt. "I get that he's trying to protect his family. But would you say he does it to a normal degree?"

Susan had rubbed her eyes and smeared her mascara. Now she took a moment to clean up with a tissue before staring at me hard. "Abnormal?" she guessed, as if that was the expected answer.

I assured her it wasn't for me to judge, "...But you did say he gets a little paranoid now and then."

"Oh, yeah. Because of that bitch, Claire. He said she tried to stab him with a steak knife. Another time she poured hot soup on his lap—on purpose."

"And now he owes her money."

"Yes! And she doesn't even need it! We're just scraping by, but she'll have him arrested for back payments if she finds us. She hates him that much."

"So that's why you move around so much."

"You know about that?"

"Your dad told me."

"Oh? Did he also tell you Mike changed our name?"

I said, "No," casually enough, but my imagination was showing me a police line-up with Mike Swenson front and center.

"Oh, yeah. After Jacksonville."

Jacksonville had preceded Norristown, I recalled. And since missing people often rely on the help of relatives, the name change would make connecting them to Susan's father much more difficult.

"Oh?" I remarked, but now my voice sounded tight. "What was your name before?"

Susan made a sour face. "Cotaldi. Sue, Mike and Johnny Cotaldi."

I opened my mouth to ask the damning question, "Do you think...?" but controlled the impulse before I spoke.

Susan noticed. "What?" she pressed.

"Nothing," I fibbed through suddenly parched lips. "I should be getting home to my dog." That convenient excuse.

Susan didn't look any different; but even if she happened to be as clueless as she seemed, she might have heard my unspoken words in her head.

Which meant that one evening, maybe in a week or a month, some night when the Swenson dinner-conversation stalls, the words might come out. "Guess what, honey. Our babysitter thinks you're a crook."

That evening might also be tonight.

Chapter 34

KNOWING THAT the Swensons had formerly been the Cotaldis gave my suspicions their first foothold, and now I was jumpy-nervous about what else I would learn.

Too impatient to cook, I ate cheese and fresh bread for dinner washed down with herbal tea. While the summer sky faded to its evening pastels, I supervised Fideaux's last outing, then stalled a little longer getting ready for bed before finally settling down at Rip's old PC. Very soon the house would be black as a tunnel, but no matter. Spies and ghosts did their best work under cover of night.

Did I really want to do this? I wondered one last time.

Well, yes. Anybody can research anything these days, and unless they're a suspect, a movie star, or a politician, chances are good their search will remain anonymous. In other words, if nothing scarier than a vindictive ex-wife showed up, I could forget about the Swensons' personal business and continue to babysit Jack with a clear conscience. On the other hand, if Mike turned out to be a fugitive, for Jack's sake, my own, and—as I optimistically believed—Susan's too, I needed to know.

The first item I found was the current couple's wedding notice, which I already knew occurred in Minneapolis without Father George in attendance. The item was short and useless except for providing Michael's middle initial, K, and the fact that the newlyweds planned to reside locally.

For lack of specifics, looking into Mike's original marriage took longer, but I eventually learned that he and

Claire wed in Bowler, Minnesota. Logical, since someone stuck in a bad marriage usually found comfort in nearby arms. Also, the newspaper write-ups confirmed that the weddings occurred three and a half years apart, a reasonable amount of time for a couple to become disenchanted, get divorced, and give it another go.

After that, I ricocheted from one website to another, partly due to natural curiosity, mostly due to my questionable research skills. I watched an interview about a celebrity bowling match that focused primarily on the peanut butter and jelly sandwich the sports figure was eating. I found a company that built bowling alleys, and a pediatric cardiologist named Bowler. I took a virtual tour of a resort offering fishing and campfires under the stars, and learned that the temperature in Bowler was presently a cool sixty-four degrees. Crisp for summer, but northern Minnesota was, after all, *north*.

Another hour of perusing useless newspaper archives for crimes Michael Costaldi might have committed gave me a headache and one more idea.

Implementing said idea, however, required phoning Bowler, Minnesota, and one of my many shortcomings is time zones. I once tried to wish Didi happy birthday while she was vacationing in Hawaii at what—for her—was three-thirty in the morning. Since then, I've been extra careful calling anywhere west of Pittsburgh. Eleven AM tomorrow seemed a safe enough hour for Minnesota, but I still wasn't entirely sure.

Then I remembered that police stations are always open.

"Bowler Police. What is your emergency?"

"I, uh, don't have an emergency. Is there another number I can call to ask a question?"

A moment later I had a bored sergeant on the line who almost sounded happy to chat. I told him my suspicions about Michael Cotaldi and what Susan described as his "paranoia."

"Interesting," remarked the sergeant, whose name was Ringwald. "But lots of people are cautious after a divorce. That doesn't make him a criminal."

"He also changed the family name after Jacksonville, and I think he might be following me."

There, I'd said it all.

In the ensuing silence I could hear Ringwald breathe. "How are you connected to these people?" he asked.

"I'm babysitting their son." I explained about meeting George and how that led to the job.

"Give me your cell number," Ringwald instructed. "I'll get back to you."

***

THE NEXT DAY'S forecast called for eighty-five degrees with a low stratus cloud cover, which meant exercising outdoors would soon feel as if you were trapped under a bowl that just came out of the dishwasher. Since dogs have needs regardless of the weather, I herded Fideaux into the car and arrived at the park's lower path before nine.

"Here you go, sport," I said as I unleashed him thirty yards in. He would stop and go, stop and go as he paused to read his p-mail, while I maintained a steady pace for whatever cardio-vascular benefit that had to offer.

The greenery seemed especially beautiful today. A broad swath of skunk cabbage adorned the creekside with its wide, rhubarb-like leaves. Overhead, the oak and beech trees canopied the underbrush fifty feet below. I especially enjoyed the dappled white trunks of a stand of sycamores and the wild white roses at their feet.

A few other cars had parked before me, so I would not have the place to myself.   Still, the path was far from crowded. I passed one woman and her two gray-muzzled mutts near the first bridge over the creek.

"Good morning," we said in turn. "Aren't we smart to beat the heat?"

Fideaux had bounded ahead, nose high, his short, curly gray coat almost ghostly in the morning light. He flashed me his best doggy smile from twenty yards away, and I knew he would be happy for the rest of the day.

After the sycamores and the third bridge, we approached the opening in the boxwood hedge. I thought I saw motion on the other side; but behind me Fideaux sniffed a weed unperturbed, and that was good enough for me.

I sidled through the opening and, wham, fell to the ground. My head hit a rock. Sparklers flared behind my eyes, then the world went black.

When I came to, everything looked blurry, and the noise in my ears sounded like water rushing through a pipe.

Also, a man lay across me as if he were doing push-ups and I was his matt. His face was way too close, and his hands…What was he doing with his hands?

"Rape!" I shouted. "Rape!"

I tried to push him off, but he was way too heavy. Also, we were stuck between the dense boxwood branches the huge rock on my right.

Where was everybody else? *Where was Fideaux?*

"Yeeow!"

Fideaux had quit growling in order to bite the man's leg. "Oof." That was me.

Shaking his leg had caused the man's arms to give out, which dropped his dead weight entirely on me. I averted my head trying to breathe.

Curly blond hair brushed my lips, and black-rimmed glasses bumped my nose.

The Hunter. I vaguely remembered distrusting him.

"Rape!" I shouted again. "Rape!" Or was I supposed to shout "fire" so people wouldn't run the other way?

"I'm not . . ." the man protested. "You were…I just…"

I'd taken a self-defense class, but the advice regarding rape escaped me. Something about women desperately fighting to remain upright when we had better strength available on the ground—our legs.

Except how do you kick an attacker away when he's on you like ham and cheese on rye?

I did the next best thing. I reached between us for his most convenient—and most vulnerable—body part. Being shorts season, the fabric was thin and pliable, probably cotton, not even permanent press. Soft, in other words. I cupped the body part in question and...

The scream the man emitted was unlike anything I had previously heard. It was loud enough to carry into the next county, for one thing, and gut-wrenching in its fervor. And, even though the self-defense instructor recommended squeezing as long as possible, ideally until your attacker passes out, I let go.

So, apparently, had Fideaux, allowing my attacker to right himself to a mostly standing position.

"Jeez, woman," The Hunter complained. "I was trying to give you mouth-to-mouth, and you damn near killed me."

I doubted that mouth-to-mouth was actually recommended for someone who was still breathing, so I had to wonder. Did he just make that up because he had other intentions?

Hearing footfalls up ahead, I sat up in time to see another man lope away, chased by The Hunter's German Shorthaired and my scruffy, clueless mutt.

I'd gotten it wrong. Very, very wrong, and it chilled me to think what my real attacker might have done if no one else had come along. Nothing good, that was for sure.

Still breathing hard, The Hunter gallantly helped me to my feet. He had also seen the other man leave, and he was smart enough to whistle his dog back.

"You dizzy or anything?" he asked.

"I think I'm okay."

"Got your phone?"

"Forgot it." A mistake I would never make again. "You?"

He plucked at this athletic shorts. "No pockets."

I arranged my face to look like abject contrition. "I'm sorry," I said. "Really, really sorry. I was scared."

"No shit." The former New Yorker doubled over to finish catching his breath, and I noticed blood from my dog's bites dripping down his leg into his white gym sock.

"You want to sue me or anything?" I asked, tactless as ever.

My rescuer remained hunched over, but he had begun to breathe normally.

"That depends," he responded from his lowered position. "You charging me with attempted rape?"

I smiled. "Nah. It was the most action I've had in years."

The man did not smile back. He turned and limped away, his dog whimpering at his side.

Among my thoughts as I watched them depart? "I am *so* not ready to date."

Chapter 35

I THOUGHT maybe The Hunter had a point, and I should call the police when I got home. The trouble was I had no description of my attacker and couldn't remember my "witness's" name. I chose to table that dilemma until after I got my head checked. Maybe by then I'd know what to say.

My cell phone rang while I was waiting my turn at the drugstore's Urgent Care Clinic. I stepped into the empty vitamin aisle to answer.

"Ms. Barnes? Bowler police. Sergeant Ringwald speaking."

With my aching head, my first thought was that one of my kids had been in a terrible accident. Garry, perhaps, washed overboard from a yacht off Nantucket. Chelsea, mugged by an irate next door neighbor.

"I looked into that guy, Michael Cotaldi," the sergeant from Bowler, Minnesota, reported.

"Omigod!" I exclaimed. "What did he do?"

Ringwald said it would take a few days to verify the facts.

"Fine, then tell me what *might* he have done."

I could hear the man's mental wheels clicking from cog to cog. "You're a civilian," he said aloud. "If you don't know what Cotaldi allegedly did, you can't accidentally tip him off."

"Wouldn't it be safer if I knew what not to say?"

Ringwald sighed.

"Just stay away from the guy. Okay? Don't go anywhere near him."

"Why not? Is he dangerous?'"

I imagined Ringwald clenching his teeth, his jaw muscles rolling.

"You can trust me," I argued. "I called you first."

Ringwald snorted out a skeptical grunt, but he finally told me what I wanted to know.

Simultaneously, the nurse called my name, so I stuck my head around the corner to give her a wave.

"...But you do nothing, you hear me?" Ringwald insisted. "Nothing! Let the professionals handle this. Stay away from the Cotaldis or Swensons or whatever they're calling themselves these days. You got that? I mean it."

"Right," I agreed because he was in Minnesota, and I was here. However, I was pretty sure if I begged off babysitting Jack, paranoid Mike would be absolutely certain I was onto him.

Onto his past, that was. Although it seemed pretty likely Cotaldi was watching, aka stalking, me. I had yet to see that person's face—not even today—so I couldn't swear it was him. One might even argue that The Hunter had actually knocked me down and, arriving late, the running man chose to steer clear. Not everybody sees themselves as a rush-in-to-rescue-the-lady hero. And come to think of it, it was a man's scream everybody in the vicinity heard.

"Thank you for your concern, Sergeant," I told Ringwald. "And thank you for looking into this so quickly."

"Tell you the truth, I thought you were nuts, no offense. But I got a buddy in Minneapolis, so I rang him up. Uh, one more thing," he prompted. "Cotaldi's address. Nothing's on the books."

"Oh dear," I stalled, "I'm not home right now, and I don't want to get it wrong."

"You   don't   remember?"   Ringwald   sounded appropriately surprised.

"If you knew where I am right now you'd understand."

"Where are you?"

I waved to a woman reaching for a bottle of cough medicine. "Will you please tell this man where I am?" I held out my phone.

"The drug store?" she said toward my fist.

Urgent Care, I mouthed then showed her the lump on the back of my head.

"Uh, Urgent Care," the woman repeated with mounting distress.

"I'm sorry, Sergeant. I fell walking in the woods this morning. Until a doctor checks me out I wouldn't be confident telling you my mother's name."

"But you've got the address, right?"

"Written down at home. Yep."

"You'll call me back as soon as you can."

"MS. BARNES," the store intercom announced.

"You bet," I assured Ringwald.

"Promise?" I think he asked just as I hung up.

He had claimed they needed a couple days to verify the facts, but what if they didn't? With luck I'd just bought myself enough time for a quick face-to-face with George Donald Elliot.

Chapter 36

STRIDING TOWARD ME from his car, George's face made Mt. Rushmore look like a sandcastle.

No greeting. No eye contact. Did he already know what I was going to say, or was he merely worried to death?

"Let's sit here," I suggested, gesturing toward some empty picnic tables shaded by red and white umbrellas. Inside the pizza place would be air-conditioned, but this conversation required privacy.

"How do you like your pizza?" I asked as I deposited my purse and phone on the table.

No answer.

After knocking on the sliding glass window displaying a menu, I told the woman who responded, "A plain personal pizza and one with all your vegetables. And two Cokes, please, lots of ice." Ice wouldn't last long out here. I was flushed and perspiring already.

Claiming a spot in the umbrella's shadow a discreet distance from my guest, I tried to gather my thoughts.

My cell phone went off. Chelsea. It killed me to do it, but I hung up.

When I leaned toward George, he finally looked my way.

No reason not to be blunt.

"Jack is Mike's son," I stated. "His natural son. Mike took him from the mother right after he and Susan married. The day they left for Indiahoma to be exact."

George's narrowed eyes squinted off into the distance. "And how do you know this?"

"Internet." The shortest answer would do for now. "Is it what you suspected?"

Susan's father drew in a deep breath, blew out the word "No" with his exhale.

"Do you think Susan knows?"

George's angry glance said, "Of course not," "How dare you?" and "What are you playing at here?" all at once.

I tented my fingers in front of my lips. Watched a blue pickup roll by on the road. Noticed a single cloud dangling in the noontime sky.

"Susan will be viewed as an accomplice, you know. She's going to need an attorney."

"Is that what the police told you?"

I hesitated long enough for him guess the answer.

"You haven't called them have you? You want Jack to stay here just as much as I do."

Not exactly.

Well, maybe.

Oh, sure.

My face must have conveyed all that, but George didn't notice.

"What if I paid you to forget about this?" he offered. "A private business transaction just between you and me."

Since no bookmaker in his right mind would believe Susan bought Mike's adoption story, whatever it was, I wasn't surprised that her father didn't trust the vagaries of the court. The surprise was that he tried to buy me off.

I waved my head no, but George wasn't finished. "If Jack really is Mike's son, wouldn't he be just as entitled to the boy as Claire?"

I was still waving my head. Couldn't seem to stop. "I don't know the circumstances of the divorce, but I do know the judge's ruling. Mike broke the law, George. He took Jack from his mother and transported him across state lines.

I looked it up. That's parental kidnapping, in Pennsylvania 'interfering with the custody of a child'. He'll do jail time for that, either in Minnesota or here, whatever the authorities work out."

George closed his eyes. His knee began to bounce.

I said I really wished I could help Susan, "but even if Mike kept her in the dark with some phony adoption paperwork, she's still going to need a good lawyer."

George was up and moving.

"What're you doing?"

"Warning Susan." The same foolish thing I would do. His cell phone was probably back in his car, charged up and ready to go.

"Don't!" I shouted, awkwardly extricating myself from the picnic bench. "Please don't. They'll run. You might never see Susan or Jack again."

Ding! The one-note text alert from my phone shot my heartrate into the stratosphere. Had to be Chelsea trying another way to reach me, but what could I do from here? I squeezed my eyes shut for a millisecond and willed her to be okay.

George had arrived at his car. I hustled closer to be sure he'd hear.

"It's too late," I told him. "I already called the police."

"Yo, you down there!" The pizza lady trying to deliver our lunch.

George opened his passenger door and reached inside.

"Please, George, don't. I think I can fix this, but you just..."

"Hey!" The pizza lady sounded pissed. Of course she did. Her customers seemed to be running out on her.

"Oh, hell…Give me a minute."

George shut his door, and I dared to breathe.

Still, I was scared. What if I hadn't hooked him with my "think I can fix this" malarkey?

I turned back. Patted the air. Assured him one more time. "I've got this. Don't phone. I've got this."

He folded his arms, no phone in his hand that I could see.

While digging pizza money out of my purse, I sneaked a glance at my message. Chelsea's name and "URGENT!!" showed on the screen. I way dying to call her back, but I'm no Super Hero. One crisis at a time for me.

"No change," I told the lady at the window.

Curiosity must have won George over, because he strolled back toward me, chin high, hands in his pockets.

"Exactly how are you going to *fix this*?" he demanded when we stood face to face.

Looking up into those gray, insurance-salesman eyes, the first thought that came to mind was, "Excellent question."

Chapter 37

THE SCENT OF warm pizza, the attack in the woods, the "Urgent" text message from Chelsea, and the dilemma about Susan and Jack conspired to stall my mind like an airplane headed into a nosedive.

Yet sometimes your brain surprises you and gets the job done.

I guided George back to the picnic-table bench, urged him to sit, then looked him in the eye.

"I misled you a moment ago," I confessed. "I did speak to the Bowler, Minnnesota, police, but I was waiting to see a doctor and balked at giving them the address until after I got home."

"Have you been home?"

"No."

George didn't seem to comprehend the favor I was doing for him and Susan, because he said, "I'm sure they have ways of getting it themselves."

"Probably," I agreed, "but Mike goes to pretty great lengths not to be found. Out-of-state area codes on their cells, for instance, and no landline. A rented house. It wouldn't surprise me if he cut a private deal with the property owner just to stay off the grid."

"I don't get it. You balk at having Mike arrested, but you don't want me to alert Susan."

"What will they do if you tell her Mike stole Jack from his mother?"

"They'll run."

"Yep. Like the wind. You may never see Jack or Susan again."

I've never seen a face go red so fast. I thought George might choke on his own blood. "Then what...why...?" Words deserted him.

To calm myself I glanced toward the road traffic, imagined the drivers delivering furniture, shopping for socks, not one of them aware of a life-changing conversation happening a head-turn away.

When I felt composed enough, I said, "It's always bothered me that adopting Jack seemed like a one-sided decision. I kept watching Susan for some sign that I was wrong."

George was too dumbstruck to comment, so I plowed ahead.

"All I saw was a young woman struggling to work out who she was. Nothing out of the ordinary; we all have to do it."

George's lips compressed into a tight line as if he were struggling not to fly apart.

"I also got the feeling she's been manipulated, probably even used."

George's chest heaved, but he managed to say, "You still haven't told me why you withheld the address."

"I haven't? I thought I did." I shrugged. "When this is over, I want Susan free to be whoever she decides to be."

"Exactly how do you plan to arrange that?" White patches had appeared on his cheeks. He kneaded his thighs with stiff fingers without looking at me. Without looking at anything.

I told him, "I'm not. You and Susan are."

"Dammit, woman..."

"You're going to hire a really good lawyer, somebody capable of negotiating with the Bowler District Attorney on your daughter's behalf—her freedom for Mike's location. When that's arranged—before the end of the day probably would be best—Susan will call the Minnesota police herself and turn Mike in."

George's bouncing knee had a mind of its own. He gazed toward the restaurant's dumpster or Hawaii, hard to tell which.

"It'll end their marriage." He twisted his head to give me a sly look that appeared to contain pleasure.

"It sure will," I agreed.

That elicited a snort and a chuckle that dispelled some of the tension.

"You busy tomorrow?" I inquired, which netted one of those head-shaking eye rolls I get every now and then.

"Why?"

"Because Jack's babysitter is going to call in sick."

"Oh."

I stood. George needed to get cracking on his attorney assignment; and if I didn't call Chelsea back in the next thirty seconds, I was going to develop hives.

George rose and shook my hand. With his longer legs he was back at his car before I could count to five.

"Hey! You forgot your pizza," I called after him.

No response.

I dialed my daughter.

Chapter 38

"CISSIE'S really hurt," Chelsea blurted before George's sedan slipped into the afternoon traffic. "I need help, Mom. Can you come? Like—right now!"

"Ronald?"

"Yeah."

"Should you call an ambulance?"

"Cissie says that'll make him even madder."

I didn't care if Ronald got so angry his head exploded; but Cissie had to live with the bastard, so she had the final say.

"Eric?" I suggested. He could help get her to the Emergency Room much faster.

"Oh, no no no…"

"On my way."

This was precisely the worst-case scenario some frightened part of me imagined the day Eric, Cissie, and I had lunch on the Voight's back steps. I wanted to hammer my fists and kick like a brat having a tantrum, but I was driving so I bottled it all up. I don't know how I arrived at my daughter's without incident.

Chelsea lurched into my arms the second I stepped inside the door. Tears pooling in her eyes, she gestured me into the living room where Cissie sat on the sofa.

Nothing about the young mother resembled the trusting, naïve woman I'd so recently met. Her face was ashen, her eyes dull. Despite her obvious pain, she sat stiffly upright holding baby Caroline snugly to her shoulder.

Approaching slowly, I stretched out my hands. "May I?"

Cissie didn't seem to understand the question.

After I gently relieved her of the sleeping child, she clutched her ribs and curled into herself.

I passed Caroline over to Chelsea. "Did you give Cissie any painkillers?"

"Not yet. I didn't want to interfere with what the doctor will do. Anyway, she's nursing, so..."

"Good thinking, Chel."

I kneeled down to Cissie's level and spoke softly. "We need to get you to a doctor. Will you let us call an ambulance?" Still the best option in my opinion.

Cissie's hand shot out and grabbed my wrist. "No ambulance. Please. No ambulance." The fear in her voice gave me chills.

"Okay, okay," I promised. She wasn't gasping for breath or bleeding anywhere I could see.

"Nothing's broken," she insisted. "I walked over here by myself."

"Is Ronald still home?"

Negative.

"Do you have your purse?"

Cissie tucked her head under her arm and sobbed.

"Okay. No problem." If necessary, I would break a window to get it.

Brow pinched with concern, Chelsea swayed from foot to foot as she rocked the baby in her arms. She was rattled, I knew, still close to tears.

"You be okay for a few minutes?"

She said yes, and I had to trust she meant it.

My hope was that Cissie had left through her backdoor and it would still be unlocked.

It was, but I turned the knob with trembling fingers. Ronald may have returned by now.

Once inside, I glanced around as if he might jump out of a shadow or drop down from the ceiling.

Nothing moved that I could hear, yet the whole house seemed to hold its breath.

Dirty dishes filled the kitchen sink, crumbs littered the vinyl tablecloth, laundry overflowed from a basket on the floor. Yet everything felt different. The odor of fear-sweat mingled with the smell of bacon grease.

I checked the stove. Off. The coffee pot. Unplugged.

Then I made my way through the dining room, glanced into the living room, and gasped.

An overstuffed chair had been knocked askew. Two top-heavy, wrought iron floor lamps I'd noticed before had toppled, their glass globes nothing but shards. A blonde-wood coffee table tilted on a broken leg. Something ceramic had exploded against a wall. The hook for the dolphin mobile above Caroline's Pack N Play had snapped. So much angry energy lingered I could almost hear Ronald's insults, helplessly watch the body punches, the vicious kicks, the final violent shove across the room.

Remaining with such a man was madness, yet I knew women did it again and again. Until now Cissie had done it, too, but maybe this time her husband had gone too far. Maybe this time she could be persuaded to heed the handwriting on the wall.

I found her purse among the rubble and checked inside for a health-insurance card. Then I ran upstairs to Caroline's room, threw extra diapers into the diaper bag by the changing table.

"Abington Emergency room, here we come," I called as I rushed back through Chelsea's front door.

"Infant seat," the injured woman warned from her prone position.

"Covered!" I fished Cissie's keys out of her purse and tossed them to my daughter. "Chelsea will drive Caroline in your car, and you'll ride with me."

I desperately wanted to counsel the young mother, persuade her to try the Women's Shelter for at least a night or two, but I simply could not. She was too traumatized to think half an hour ahead, in too much pain to think at all. I let her rest in the backseat with a pillow.

After I gave the receiving nurse some basic information, the emergency staff whisked Cissie away on one of their many wheelchairs. I wouldn't see her again for over an hour.

Chelsea arrived with Caroline in her car-seat carrier, but one glance at the waiting room's revolving cast of needed and needy and my daughter waved me outside. The afternoon heat was at its apex, but an overhang sheltered the unloading zone from the sun. We chose a bench away from the door and flopped down gratefully.

Caroline fell asleep sucking on a purple pacifier, and I finally got to ask what happened.

Chelsea leaned back and sighed. "I was watering my hanging baskets before it got too hot. A little before noon I guess, so I was on my front porch when Cissie ran out.

"Ronald shouted for her to 'Get back in here,' but Cissie just stood there, so he came out after her. He was shoving her toward the steps when Eric stormed out of his house yelling to let her go.

"Ronald told him to mind his own business, so Eric threatened to call the police.

"That's when Ronald pushed Cissie aside and squared off in front of Eric.

"'Go ahead,'" he says. 'I'll tell them what you did to dear old Granny.'

"Eric started to laugh that off, but Ronald was serious, so Eric told him he was crazy, that he hadn't done anything to Maisie.

"'Oh, yeah? That's not what her doctor thinks.

"Until then Cissie'd just been biting her thumb and listening, but Ronald's zinger made her gasp. 'I didn't,' she tried to tell Eric, but then she saw Ronald's face. The guy was steaming, Mom. He looked like he wanted to punch Cissie right then and there.

"Eric must have been pretty alarmed, too, because he tried to calm things down. 'The doctor's wrong,' he said. 'I would never hurt Maisie.'

"'Oh, yeah?' Ronald challenged him. 'Then how come you told my wife you'd be better off without the old bag?'

"That really upset Eric. He called Ronald a liar, and I was sure fists would fly. But they didn't. For some reason Eric backed off..."

My daughter lowered her head and spread her hands. "...which must have been exactly what Ronald wanted, because he gave Cissie the smuggest, most arrogant look I've ever seen. She got the message, too, whatever it was, because she practically wilted.

"Then Ronald turned back to Eric and said he guessed it was his word against Eric's—'except for one thing.' He's got a witness who saw Eric man-handling Maisie into his car. She was fighting back tooth and nail, hollering and slapping at Eric. Even worse, it happened the day before Maisie fell down the stairs, Mom. Ronald said he remembered because it rained and he had gotten off work."

Unfortunately, that sounded true.

I asked Chelsea if she knew why Ronald had come home in the first place.

She nodded. "To check up on Cissie, who happened to be on the phone."

"With…?"

"A girlfriend, but Ronald thought she was talking to Eric. That's why he exploded."

"She told you this?"

"Yes. While we were waiting for you."

I didn't want to disillusion my daughter, but I couldn't imagine how Eric would have known Cissie was in trouble if they hadn't been on the phone together. Also, even a Neanderthal like Ronald would know how to access the most recent caller's name and number.

I did not believe Eric got that 'better off without the old bag' line from Cissie. Surely, she knew better than to ever mention Eric's name to her husband.

Yet somehow Ronald had either discovered, or invented, another way to tighten his chokehold on her. Whether Cissie and Eric were friends or lovers didn't especially matter. Ronald felt entitled to do whatever he wished to his wife.

Chapter 39

BABY CAROLINE had been fussing for her afternoon meal, and Cissie was eager to accommodate. When she reached out for her child in the Emergency room's numbered cubicle, neither Chelsea nor I could miss seeing a broad bruise on her forearm.

In my imagination I heard Ronald's disclaimer. "She's lying, Officer. The woman is a total klutz." But that wouldn't fly this time. Even if Cissie fabricated her own "clumsy" excuse, her present injuries had surely triggered an official, "These are your resources…" speech.

"Will Mrs. Voight be staying overnight?" I inquired of the nurse who came to make notes on Cissie's chart.

"No, she's got her discharge papers and prescriptions. She's good to go whenever she's ready." The young woman cast a concerned glance toward Cissie before moving onto her next responsibility.

I pulled up one of the two chairs, gestured Chelsea into the other. Monitors pinged, and the muted bustle beyond the curtain kept us acutely aware of where we were.

Cissie reluctantly met my eye.

"What'll it be?" I pressed.

She fingered the baby's collar and gazed off into the distance, perhaps all the way into the future.

"He may hurt Caroline," I reminded her. "Maybe not today or tomorrow, but down the road. And he's hurting you now. You don't deserve to be treated like this, Cissie. Nobody does."

"I know, I know." Tears slipped down the young woman's cheeks. "But I love him."

"Understood," I conceded with a nod. Then I slipped into my own motherly aspect, the authoritative one that said, *I'm older; I know more than you.*

"When I was dating," I seemed to reminisce, "I got dumped by a lot of guys. A *lot*," I emphasized. "So many that I came up with a way to get over just about anybody."

Cissie's brow crimped. "You're kidding, right?"

I fixed her with a look that dared her not to take me seriously.

"What did you do?" My perceptive daughter prompted.

"So glad you asked. I concentrated on their faults. Really, *really* concentrated on their faults."

"And that worked?"

"You bet it did," I declared. "Everybody has faults."

Chelsea's lips twitched with mischief. "Lucky Dad didn't concentrate on yours."

"Watch it, kid." I teased, and Cissie actually smiled.

Then she abruptly turned inward. Stroked Caroline's soft hair the way you pet a kitten, to give and receive comfort. "I don't know..."

I stood, clasped my hands in front of me. "Then how about just one night. Give yourself a short break from Ronald and see what the shelter's about at the same time."

Ronald's belief in his own entitlement wouldn't disappear overnight, but his period of good behavior might last a little longer. Hopefully, long enough for Cissie to start planning a permanent escape.

Caroline had finished nursing. An aide with a wheelchair hovered nearby.

"How about it?" I asked in my most encouraging tone.

Cissie winced as she hefted her daughter into the burp position.

"Okay," she agreed. "One night."

Chapter 40

WHEN I VISITED this emergency room with Maisie Zumstein after her fall, the notice in the women's restroom asking, "Are you a victim of abuse?" or "Are you afraid of your partner?" had caught me off guard. Now I recognized it for a hand extended to pull someone out of hell, or the key to unlock a prison door.

After programming the number into my phone, I hurried outside for privacy and a reliable signal. Trotting across the driveway to a tree-shaded sidewalk, I waved to Chelsea, waiting for the valet parker to retrieve our cars. Cissie and Caroline rested behind her on one of the benches.

Natalie, the shelter manager who answered my call, sounded young and competent. I sketched out the situation as best I could, adding with regret that Cissie only agreed to leave her husband for one night.

"It's a start," the manager reassured me. She suggested we meet at a certain corner of an Acme supermarket parking lot. "I'll be driving a green van."

"We need a few minutes to pick up a prescription, and maybe some lunch."

She told me she'd be there in twenty minutes, "and I'll wait."

My, "Thank you," sounded grossly inadequate.

***

I noticed Natalie surveying our surroundings before she emerged from the van to greet us. She appeared to be scarcely older than Cissie with black hair and startlingly beautiful blue eyes. She wore a pale yellow t-shirt tucked into a summer skirt and flip flops adorned with beads.

After introducing herself with a smile, she cautioned, "We shouldn't stand around too long." Addressing Cissie, she asked, "Would you like to ride with me?"

"My car's here, but I'm not supposed to drive."

Natalie nodded. "Pain meds, right?"

Cissie had confided to Chelsea and me that three of her ribs were broken, and just breathing hurt like crazy.

"So here's the thing," Natalie explained. "You're welcome to have a car at the shelter; but you should realize it may be spotted if you go out."

Cissie cast a panicky glance toward her gray Subaru, and I could almost hear what she was thinking. Her car represented freedom.

"Or your husband might report it stolen," Natalie added. "We can give the police a heads up to avoid that, but it might be best to let your friends park it back at your place. What do you think? It's up to you."

"I'd like to have it with me," Cissie insisted.

"Okay. Then everybody follow me." Natalie climbed back into her van and waited while everybody else got belted in. This time Chelsea drove Cissie's car with Caroline and Cissie on board. I trailed along in my own car.

A few minutes into our drive, a terrifying thought came over me. Mike Swenson. Never mind that I wasn't certain he'd been tailing me. The truth was I'd been too distracted by everything else to check my surroundings, and the realization made my heart hammer and my palms sweat. The last thing I wanted was expose Cissie, or anybody else, to more danger.

If I'd started out twitchy nervous, now I was hyper-vigilant. Every plain black sedan potentially belonged to Mike, and the roads were overrun with black sedans. Left, right, front, and back. I saw them by the dozens until I was nearly crazed with concern.

Natalie's route led through the close-packed suburbs west of Philadelphia, where shopping centers and strip malls and big box stores were plentiful, and housing just as dense. Only when we reached the countryside and thinner traffic could I feel certain that Swenson/Cotaldi wasn't along for the ride.

At last we turned into a long, crushed-stone driveway ending at a sprawling blue farmhouse. Three or four cars were parked around back, but the green van stopped out front.

While the shelter manager and Chelsea helped Cissie and Caroline, I lagged behind to calm myself and take in the place.

The curling black roof shingles and peeling paint underscored the organization's lack of funds, while an inviting row of red impatiens in industrial-sized coffee cans bloomed on each porch step. Off to the left, a blonde girl pumped and kicked a tree swing for all it was worth. A barefoot boy of about three sat splay-legged in a sandbox shoveling his way toward China. Their mother supervised from a blanket in the shade, but even in deep shadow the sling on her right arm was plainly visible.

Distressing enough, but it was the wheelchair ramp leading to the porch that drained the last of my emotional reserve. It reminded me that abuse has no age limit and that even young victims like Cissie might arrive unable to walk.

Natalie noticed my body language and shot me an understanding glance.

Embarrassed, I made a show of reaching inside the car for my purse. Only when the others were safely inside would I wipe my eyes and blow my nose. I'd had a short night, a frightening morning in the woods, a difficult lunch with George—all before this episode with Cissie. Add to that my fears about Mike Swenson, and my mood could only be described as grim.

Natalie emerged from the house and caught me using a tissue.

"You did good," she said as she sauntered over. "You got her here. That's enough."

I gestured with the tissue before putting it in my pocket. "The wheelchair ramp got me," I confessed.

"Hard to fathom, I know."

"Why do men do it?"

She'd been leaning against my car but shoved off and began to walk. "That's a long story for another time," she said. "Let's just get Cissie and Caroline settled in, okay?" She held the farmhouse door open with her foot. "There's a fan, but no air-conditioning I'm afraid."

"But they'll be safe," I remarked over the lump lodged in my throat.

"Yes," Natalie reassured me. "They'll be safe."

...for now, remained unspoken.

***

CISSIE'S TINY, THIRD-FLOOR room in the shelter had been an attic nook in the house's former life. Now it was painted a clean white and contained a single bed, a crib, a floor lamp and a rocking chair. Plastic boxes served as containers for the few possessions the new residents brought with them, perhaps their only possessions now. At the single, screened window ruffled curtains puffed in and out on the breeze.

Chelsea changed Caroline on a towel on the floor while Cissie curled uncomfortably on the bed. Now that she was safe, the toll of last night's beating and today's tough decision had caught up with her. She stared at the floor as if she were already asleep.

As soon as Caroline was settled into the crib with her toy bunny and a pacifier, Chelsea and I said our good-byes.

When we reached the first floor, I stuck my head into Natalie's office. Two other women were there, a mere teenager dusting the bookshelves, another in her fifties dozing in an armchair. I understood. My own lowest points always came when I was alone. It made sense that those with the worst nightmares would be comforted by the company of others.

Natalie was talking on the phone, guilting a grocery store manager into donating food. "You can? Thanks, Mr. Grater," she said finally. "I'll be there this afternoon. Right. Two on the dot. I don't suppose you could throw in a box of diapers? Okay. We're glad for anything you can spare." She hung up and switched her attention to Chelsea and me.

"You need food?" I inquired.

She nodded. "Getting enough to eat at home is a problem for some of these women, so I try to keep our pantry full. One less thing for them to worry about. But yes, we need everything—always."

Humbled and awed by the young woman's dedication, I thanked her for being there for Cissie. "I hope she decides to stay longer."

"I hope so, too. But be careful not to pressure her. Her husband is all about control, so we can't be."

"Of course," I assured her, but it was timely advice. I'd already begun to compile the many reasons why Cissie should stay here.

"Caroline's going to wake up soon," Chelsea mentioned, "and Cissie's due for more pain pills at three."

"Debbie, you got that?" Natalie asked of the teenager with the dust rag.

"Baby, check. Pills three o'clock," the girl repeated.

Natalie extended her hand for me to shake. "Watch your back," she urged both Chelsea and me. "Ronald may have spies in the neighborhood. If he thinks you had anything to do with Cissie leaving, it could get nasty."

"We will," I replied, but I was tired and didn't absorb the advice completely.

Natalie's brows lowered. "I'm not kidding," she warned. "Some batterers will do anything to keep what they believe is rightfully theirs."

"Anything," the teenager echoed, and I finally took the warning to heart. These women would know.

BOBBY WAS ALREADY HOME when I dropped off my daughter.

"Stay for dinner?" he offered as he and Chelsea embraced. They both looked exhausted; I knew I was.

"Thanks, but I better get going." I lusted for a mushroom omelet, some junk TV, and an early bedtime.

The languid pace of the early evening traffic forced me to relax, and by the time I turned onto Beech Tree Lane a pastel twilight softened the Eastern seaboard. Nestled in among summer-fat bushes, the modest red rancher Rip and I had loved at first sight looked more beautiful to me than the Taj Mahal.

Yet after I parked by the front walk and switched off the engine, the events of the day conspired to make me uneasy. I scoured my surroundings as best I could yet noticed nothing amiss. Still I was loathe to leave the car.

"Chicken," I scolded myself as I climbed out. I was a woman living alone; I'd had moments like this before and would surely experience more.

I locked the car with the clicker on my key chain, but, to mollify my jangled nerves, threaded the keys between my fingers like pointy brass knuckles. If I was being silly, nobody would ever know.

"Hey!" yelled an angry voice that shot my pulse into the stratosphere. "Stop right there!"

Still wearing the dirt-crusted jeans and heavy boots from work, Ronald Voight had emerged from the pickup truck in

front of my next-door neighbor's. Slamming the door behind
him, he overtook me before I'd run five paces. Grabbed my
arm. Blocked my way.

"Where is my wife?" Nostrils flaring, he crowded so
close I smelled his sweat, saw the veins pounding in his
temples.

"I...I don't know."

"Liar! Where...is...my...wife?"

Stepping even closer, he grabbed my shoulders and
shook.

Inside the house Fideaux frantically growled and barked.
A shame I couldn't open the door to let him vent his fury—
and mine.

"Tell the truth, bitch, or so help me..." He raised his fist.

"Let her go," a male voice commanded. "The police are
on their way."

Voight spun to direct fresh rage at the newcomer. "Why
you..."

I tried to run.

Voight grabbed my hair.

I raked his arm with my keys. He let go, but I was off-
balance and landed on my butt.

With a last piercing glare Ronald turned toward the
balding, older man, whom I now recognized as the census-
taker. Backing up, he raised his clipboard as if to protect his
head, but Ronald plowed him down and kept going. Climbed
into his pickup. Roared away.

Pen poised for action, my rescuer scurried into the street,
but just as quickly returned.

"Didn't get the license."

"Doesn't matter," I assured him as I dusted myself off.
"The guy lives next door to my daughter."

"He does?"

"Yes."

Both still jacked on adrenaline, we gravitated toward the house, where Fideaux was still sounding off.

Inserting the proper key, I warned my rescuer to brace himself. "...uh, what's your name again?"

"John. John Butler."

"Ginger Barnes." Shaking his pillowy hand, I clasped my left over his right for emphasis. "Thank you for saving me, John Butler. You couldn't have come at a better time."

When we stepped inside, Fideaux twirled and leapt with joy. The man who scared his person was gone. He was free to rudely sniff the stranger and step on his shoes.

I asked whether the police were actually coming.

"I'm afraid there wasn't time," Butler admitted. "Shall we call them now?"

I gestured us into the living room. "That's up to you. I just fell down trying to scratch the bastard. You're the one who got shoved."

"Assault. I see it on my list every day, but I never thought it would happen to me."

"What list is that?"

"I'm conducting a crime survey. We follow up every six months for two years by phone, but the initial interview has to be in person. That's why I'm here. You're one of my random subjects."

"And I've been a pain in the ass, haven't I? Sorry. I thought you were a regular census-taker, and I didn't think it was time for that."

"We wrote you a letter."

My eyes strayed to a large basket of unopened mail, mostly junk, but apparently not all.

John Butler strolled over, rummaged through the heap, selected an envelope, and presented it to me.

"Sorry," I apologized again. "It looked a little like it was from Publishers Clearinghouse."

"Under the circumstances, I'm glad you were so cautious about a man on your doorstep. Does this sort of thing happen to you often?" He tilted his chin toward the front yard.

"No. Is that a question from your survey, or are you just asking?"

"Just me," he answered. "For now."

I settled onto the chair at the right of the empty fireplace. My guest took the other. He was cute when he smiled, even had a dimple in his left cheek. I was relieved to notice he wore a wedding band.

"You said you knew the man?"

I described my recent acquaintance with Voight's wife and how Chelsea and I had helped get her to the shelter.

Chelsea!

"Mind if I take a minute to call my daughter?"

"Of course not."

Bobby answered, which was probably best. He could warn Chelsea about their hot-headed neighbor without sounding like a mother.

I sketched in the details.

"Omigod, are you alright?" Bobby exclaimed, then peppered me with questions like, "How did Ronald even know where you live?"

It took me a moment to think. "I may have told him myself the day we met."

"Your address?"

"No, the town. But I'm in the phone book." I would be correcting that ASAP.

"Did you report the incident? You should, you know."

That I had thought about already. Since I wasn't hurt, and since Ronald believed the census man had already called it in, I worried that making a formal complaint might provoke Cissie's husband even more. "...Of course, if Mr. Butler wants to report his assault, I'll back him up."

He waved his head no.

"Please be really careful, okay?" I urged my son-in-law. "Both of you, please."

"You, too, uh, Gin," he responded, cementing both my mother-in-law name and our mutual bond.

When I returned to my seat, John Butler wore a cat-ate-the-canary smile.

"What?" I asked bluntly. This was the end of a very long day.

Pen in hand, clipboard resting on his lap, the census-taker got down to business. "Mrs. Barnes," he opened with a bemused tilt to his chin. "During the past six months, have you been the victim of a crime?"

Chapter 42

NATALIE PHONED me from the women's shelter the next morning. Cissie had had an especially rough night and clearly needed more time to heal. "I think I've talked her into staying a little longer, but she needs a few more things from home, one thing in particular. Any chance you can drop them off?"

I said, "Of course!" and Natalie recited a list.

As soon as we hung up, I realized why my gut felt clenched. Invading Ronald territory was not a good idea. Especially not alone.

Eric answered my call with a hangover groan. Yesterday hadn't exactly been a walk in the park for him either.

I explained my assignment, adding, "If you're willing, a little backup would be greatly appreciated."

Eric took a moment to rub his whiskers and clear his throat.

I couldn't fault him for stalling. If the neighborhood spy alerted Ronald someone was in his home and Ronald happened to be working nearby…

"Yeah, sure. What the hell," Eric agreed anyway.

We would simply have to get the job done before anything awful could happen.

"Aspirin?" I suggested to see if I was right about the hangover.

"Oh yeah."

***

WHEN I ARRIVED at Chelsea's forty minutes later, my daughter was emptying the dishwasher. Sipping black coffee at the kitchen counter, Eric flinched when two pots she was putting away clanked.

"Sorry," Chelsea told him.

"De nada, Coach."

To complement his stage-fright therapy, Will Miller had advised the singer to secure a voice coach. "No point in being mentally ready if your instrument isn't tuned!" was how he put it. Already invested in Eric's success, Chelsea was also convenient, and affordable. She made certain of it. Seeing the two of them interact so comfortably confirmed that the arrangement was working out well.

Yet I fell silent and clenched my teeth anyway. Exactly why I could not say. Nobody could prove Eric had done anything wrong, but I still felt uneasy around him.

So the problem was probably me. Now and then I tend to be overly suspicious. And maybe I haven't quite shed my lioness instincts when it comes to my cubs. Logic insisted that Eric had no earthly reason to shove either Chelsea or me down a flight of stairs, and I was a logical person. Right? Up to me to give him the benefit of a doubt.

"Shall we go?" he suggested, resting his empty mug on the counter.

"Why not?"

The most inconspicuous route to the Voight's backdoor was a gap in the hedge. After we squeezed through, I retrieved the key I'd been told was on a nail inside the gardening shed while Eric surveyed our surroundings.

He halted just inside the kitchen door. "What's that smell?"

I hadn't noticed anything different from the day before, but now that he mentioned it…I lifted the lid of the trash can at the end of the counter.

"Roses." About a dozen battered red ones mingled with the kitchen garbage. Also, a nearly empty Gordons gin bottle sat on the table where it hadn't been before.

Eric had moved on. "What're we looking for?" he wondered as he regarded the mess.

"Diapers, breast pump, stuff like that." I didn't mention the special item. Don't know why.

"Sorry I asked."

He held one of the trash bags I'd brought along as I gathered a fuzzy blue elephant from the Pack N Play, a couple of light baby blankets, pacifiers, Cissie's phone charger. The living room had been righted somewhat—the glass swept off the floor, the lamps set out of the way—yet the broken coffee table remained, and the stuffed chair and other items were still displaced enough to give the room a disturbing vibe. When I mentioned that most of what I needed was upstairs," Eric said, "Thank goodness."

Heated by the summer sun, Baby Caroline's room was thick with odors, stale air, used diapers, the cloying fragrance of lotion. I ransacked the dresser we'd brought up from the basement with the haste of a thief.

Eric rocked on his heels and overlooked the street. "The spy left," he remarked with a lift of his eyebrow.

"Do you think he saw us?"

A resigned shrug. "Dunno. His wife went, too."

"Doesn't mean he didn't warn Ronald."

Another careless shrug. "So speed it up."

I collected an envelope Cissie had hidden under the diaper pail, the primary reason I was here rather than at Kmart buying inexpensive replacements for whatever Cissie needed. Along with a small stash of cash, the envelope contained Cissie's mother's diamond engagement ring, which Natalie agreed Cissie would never see again if Ronald was clever enough to find it. I surmised that it represented her only keepsake and perhaps her only financial asset, too.

I tucked the envelope inside my waistband under my shirt.

Next, clothes for Cissie.

Her side of the joint closet was surprisingly sparse, making me wonder whether Ronald's control over his wife included a bare-minimum budget. Disliking the man more and more, I grabbed shorts and t-shirts as fast as my hands allowed and tossed them to my accomplice.

Eric reverently placed each item in the second bag. If Ronald was on his way, Eric didn't seem to care. Indeed, he seemed consumed by enough dark thoughts to fill a cave.

As we hustled back through the hedge and approached my car, naturally, my inquisitive nature forced me to ask, "So. How's it going?"

Eric stopped short. "What do you mean '*it*?'"

I tilted my head. Breathed. "Oh, just everything in general."

Eric dropped the bags into the trunk. "Like am I depressed about my grandmother? Or how do I like going to a shrink?"

I fixed him with a stare. "Just trying to break the tension. If I'm getting too personal, why not say, 'Everything's fine,' like everybody else."

"Everything's fine," he snapped, stepping into my space. "My grandmother's still dead; and Cissie, the sweetest woman I ever met, has bruises all over and three broken ribs from that sonovabitch she married. I can't find a job doing jack shit; and you and your daughter want me to sing, for God's sake. So, yes, everything's fine. Thanks for asking."

Eric slammed the trunk shut. Then he surprised me. "You know what he calls her at work, don't you?"

"No."

"The Blonde Bitch."

"That's...that's...How did she find out?"

"Company party. Somebody's wife pulled her aside and told her. Cissie said she'd been having a really good time up until then."

Waving his head, Eric set off across Chelsea's front yard toward home, and I just managed to thank him before I would have had to shout it for all the block to hear. He was still shaking his head when he disappeared inside.

I went in to say a quick good-bye to my daughter. Best to leave before the spy came home and saw it again. Ronald would connect my car with Cissie's missing clothes in a heartbeat.

Chelsea seemed to have something to say, but when I asked, "What?" a little too abruptly, she waved me off.

We hugged good-bye, but then she told me to wait a second and ducked back into the kitchen.

When she returned, she handed me a brown lunch bag. "Here. Eric left this for you."

Inside were the mysteries I'd bought for Maisie.

"Thanks."

Chelsea still seemed preoccupied, so I asked again, "Anything else?"

"No. Never mind. Go!"

I went.

Chapter 43

NATALIE SAID she liked to keep the shelter's pantry full, so on the way to deliver Cissie's necessities, I stopped at Produce Junction. The earthy smells, the colorful displays, the simple, urgent transactions all stimulated my senses—and reminded me of Jack.

The night before I'd texted Susan my lame, "terrible cold" excuse and hinted that George might babysit in my place. Susan did not write back. Now, as I waited my turn at the rough wooden counter, it occurred to me that I might never see her step-son again.

Heart-heavy and bordering on tears, I managed to deliver my, "Double potatoes, tomatoes, string beans, lettuce, onions, avocados, and oranges," spiel with dignity. Even so, the clerk seemed to distrust my composure because he gathered my order with remarkable haste.

When I arrived at the shelter, Natalie was trotting toward the green van, but she stopped and waited for me. Overhead, clouds the weight of elephants lumbered across the afternoon sky. A damp breeze messed with Natalie's long, black hair.

"Any trouble getting Cissie's stuff?" she inquired, her hands tucked in the back pockets of her jeans.

"I took a bodyguard."

"Good move."

"Yeah, well. Ronald was probably at work, but…"

"Or in jail."

My eyes widened. "I thought Cissie had to…"

"Press charges? Nope. Her injuries were clearly no accident. The hospital took pictures, and I think a police officer was already there for something else. Bottom line— the District Attorney doesn't need Cissie's testimony to prosecute."

I savored that thought as I hoisted the first box of vegetables out of the trunk.

"Wow," Natalie exclaimed. "Have you been reading my mind?"

"Just eavesdropping," I admitted. "I wish I could do more."

"Here. Let me get that."

I handed her the box and hoisted the other. "Weren't you going somewhere?"

"It can wait."

I didn't know how to begin, but Natalie didn't require words. She set her box on the ground and gestured for me to do the same. Then she leaned against the car as if she had all the time in the world.

"You want to know why some men think it's okay to beat their wives."

I nodded.

She flipped a hand toward the sky "They feel entitled," she said.

The degree of anger that welled up surprised me. I glanced away.

"Society still condones the abuse, Ms. Barnes."

I met her gaze.

She shook her finger as if beginning a list. "Religion," she stated. "Many of them still tell women to submit to their husbands."

A second finger. "MTV. A rap singer won an award for an album with a song on it about a man murdering his girlfriend—you can hear her screams in the background."

Another finger.   "The legal system—a wife-beater usually gets off easier than a guy who beat up a stranger." She ticked off examples even faster.   "Magazines, movies, comedians, stage plays all still depict abuses perpetrated against women; and, I'm sorry to say, most people don't even notice.   Watch for it," she suggested.   "You'll see what I mean."

My face was surely red, my breathing shallow.

"Even children's books have mom and the kids pampering dad to keep him from getting angry.   And pornography!"   Natalie snorted.   "Everybody knows porn demeans and objectifies women, but ask most men and I bet they'll say it was their first exposure to sex."

She looked into my dumbstruck face and frowned.   "And then there's what I call the great Get Out of Jail Free card. They're not responsible for their aggressive behavior, don't you know. Violence is in their nature."   Natalie threw up her hands.   "That's enough.   You shouldn't have gotten me started."

"But we have laws…"

Natalie wagged her head and settled back against the car. "Not until the late nineteenth century we didn't, and then only the worst offenses were addressed. Anyhow, nobody enforced anything until the 1970s, and nothing consistently until 1990."

"So we've still got men out there who feel entitled."

"Yup. Maybe their fathers beat their mothers. Maybe they were abused themselves. Vicious cycle." She lifted the box of vegetables.

I followed suit. "But…but why do women put up with it?"

She began to walk. "Batterers are devious smart, Ms. Barnes. They know what they're doing, and they know how to get away with it," she glanced over her shoulder, "starting with the right victim."

That last statement hit me right between the eyes. Cissie's insecurities did complement Ronald's inflated opinion of himself. Perhaps a major ingredient to the whole mess.

Yet there had to be a way someone could tilt her toward the Common Sense side of the fence. Just maybe it would help to determine whether Eric Zumstein was the good guy Cissie, and also my daughter, seemed so confident he was. Or, was he actually the selfish, greedy schemer part of me feared he might be?

Either way, it was information Cissie desperately needed. God forbid she should make the same mistake again.

***

NURSING CAROLINE, Cissie smiled up wanly from the attic rocking chair. The afternoon's humidity caused the room to smell like dusty wood, while the air wafting in through the open window smelled of ozone. Most likely I would be driving home from the shelter in a storm.

"How are you?" I opened, as I lowered myself onto the edge of the bed.

Cissie averted her eyes, angled her head to the side. "Been better."

I nodded. Joked that I hoped so.

She smiled at that, but in an older, worldlier way. No more ditzy, "Oh, Mrs. B! Can you help me with this?" Now I was the younger, lighter one.

"Do you mind if I ask you something personal? It's about Eric."

"I guess," she said with a tiny shrug. What was privacy to her now?

"Did the two of you talk about his grandmother?"

She shifted the child in her arms and smiled. "We talk about everything."

On the phone, or in person? Best not to ask.

I lifted an eyebrow. "Did Eric tell you why the doctor thought he had something to do with his grandmother's fall? The one that broke her hip?"

"Not really. Mostly he sounded off about the doctor. He was really pissed."

"Was it the attending physician or the surgeon? Do you remember?" Always good to be sure.

"Dr. Quinn, whichever one he was."

I allowed myself to breathe. "How about you? Do you think Eric could have hurt his grandmother?"

"No. No, never," she protested, but I'd already caught a quicksilver flash of doubt. In that respect Cissie was no more sure of Eric than I was.

"I hope not," I responded, but both of us were just tossing pennies into a fountain.

While Caroline burbled and burped, while a gust of cool air fluffed the curtain and tickled my chin, I pondered my daughter's impression of the silent sidewalk exchange between Ronald and his wife. Chelsea seemed to view the threat of reporting Eric for mistreating his grandmother as another way of controlling his wife.

"What do you think Ronald might know about Eric that we don't?" I wondered aloud.

Cissie's head jerked with alarm. "Nothing!"

"I'm not so sure, Cissie. How do you think Ronald knew about the doctor's misgivings?"

Cissie's shoulders twitched. She rolled her eyes, tossed a hand, pressed her fingers to her forehead. "I dunno. Sometimes it feels as if he's inside my head."

"How do you mean?"

"As if he hears my thoughts."

"You realize that's impossible."

"Yeah, I know, but…"

"Where were you when Eric told you about his run-in with the doctor?"

"Upstairs, I guess. On the phone."

"Did Eric call from his house?"

"From wherever he was. He wasn't with me. We're just friends. Ronald's wrong about that." Her embarrassment seemed to underscore her honesty, up to a point.

I felt my shoulders relax a little. Very little. I was thinking about bugs that monitor live phone conversations, even store them in the cloud if you have the right gadget. Also motion-activated nanny cams that catch your babysitter pilfering pocket change. Or your wife with another man. Who needs a nosy, unemployed neighbor to inform you when you've got Wi-Fi, a cheap gadget, and a mobile phone?

"What's the newest appliance in your house?"

"Appliance? I don't know. What does it matter?"

"Trust me. It matters."

"Our alarm clock, I guess. The old one broke."

I bet it did.

"Do yourself a favor. If you go home, drop the thing from a second-story window."

Cissie got it quicker than I expected.

"Not necessary," she informed me. "When I go home, I won't be talking to Eric ever again. Break the news to him, will you? I'm tired of ignoring his calls."

On my way out, the teenager who'd been dusting before caught up with me on the porch. "You're Ms. Barnes, aren't you? Natalie left this for you."

A paperback titled *Why Does He Do That?* by Lundy Bancroft. My new bedside reading.

Chapter 44

GAME ON. I didn't believe Cissie's never-going-to-speak-to-Eric-again proclamation for one second. Why? The tears in her eyes.

Also, I had just delivered her phone charger. She hadn't been ignoring anything; her phone was dead. Consequently, I had no qualms about learning whatever I could about Eric Zumstein on her behalf, especially how his grandmother died.

How to proceed was the question. Chewing on that while I was driving home, what I remembered about that Serenity Prayer by Reinhold Neibuhr came to mind. *Have the courage to change what you can, accept what you can't; and good luck figuring out which is which.*

The summer rainstorm held off until Fideaux and I were strolling up our street. Then with her tongue in her cheek, Mother Nature pelted my umbrella and the dog's hide until the gutters ran like mini rivers. Fideaux dispatched his business with grit and efficiency, and we hastened back home to our dinners.

All the while, my brain alternately poked at the Eric problem and ignored it.

With my evening decaf, I concluded Dr. Quinn was key.

By bedtime I finally quit procrastinating and picked up the phone.

His answering-service person sounded unusually perky for the hour, as if she was in a western state and had just finished supper.

I said I needed to speak to Dr. Quinn.

"Is it an emergency, because…?"

"No."

"This is his answering service," she stated from memory. "For an appointment you need to phone the office during business hours."

Since I'd procrastinated too long already, I let it all pour out. "I don't want a regular appointment. I need to know whether a woman might be leaving her violent husband for a murderer."

"Listen, lady…"

"Ginger Barnes. You can call me Gin."

"Whatever. This is an answering service. I have real people calling with real emergencies. If you don't hang up right now, I'm going to use another line to give the police your number."

She had Caller ID. Of course, she did. Who doesn't?

I pointed out that bothering the police would delay getting the information I needed from Dr. Quinn, "and I'd really like his input before my friend goes home, which might be tomorrow." I put the odds of that happening at 50/50; but it was possible, especially if Ronald hadn't yet been released on bail.

"Where are you?" I asked but didn't wait for an answer. "Never mind. Wherever it is, I bet your hospital's ladies' room displays the phone number of a women's shelter. Am I right?"

Silence, but she didn't hang up.

"I just took a woman named Cissie to our local shelter. Her husband broke three of her ribs and inflicted plenty of other damage. She has a baby daughter. She also met a neighbor, a man who is attracted to her and would love to get her out of the abusive situation. However, there's a cloud over his head regarding how his grandmother died. Dr.

Quinn was the grandmother's attending physician. I need to know whether my friend would be leaving a batterer for a murderer. Got it?"

"Yes, ma'm. I think I do."

"Will you please relay my request for a brief meeting with Dr. Quinn at your earliest convenience?"

"Yes, ma'm, I will."

Considering the week I'd had, I should have fallen asleep in my soup, but no. Anticipating a nasty call from Dr. Quinn, I twitched like a nervous bride until Fideaux left me for the living room sofa.

Too stressed to read the book Natalie lent me, I hunted down the lunch bag of mystery novels I'd bought for Maisie.

Back in bed, I propped myself against a couple of pillows, tucked my feet under the covers, and peeked inside the bag.

The pages of all four paperbacks looked tighter than crackers in a sleeve. Maisie hadn't read one word.

Or else she didn't live long enough to start. Not the sort of thought that invited sleep.

I didn't dare start a lengthy page-turner, so I pinched the skinniest book with my fingertips and slid it out of the bag.

Ick. The bottom edge had a small, dark smear, maybe breakfast jam or gravy from Maisie's dinner. Or, considering where she was, it might be blood. I set the short read aside and tried another.

Pristine. The cover depicted a sunny beachside cottage festooned with flowerboxes. As advertised, the first page was charming and light, not too ominous…

I tossed the novel aside and curled up under the covers. Staring into the dark, I played and replayed an imaginary scenario in my head until finally I fell asleep.

Five hours later my phone rang.

Chapter 45

WITH DAWN a mere hint on the horizon, I nearly swept my cell phone to the floor before I managed to say hello.

"Who are you?" Dr. Quinn demanded in a hostile, whiskey voice that slapped me wide awake.

"Somebody who wants to exchange information about Maisie Zumstein. Critical information."

"Don't play games with me, Ms. Barnes. You told my messaging service an elaborate story about an abused woman I never heard of. I fail to see what that melodrama has to do with Maisie Zumstein's death."

"Give me ten minutes this morning, and I'll tell you."

"Tell me now."

"Do you do your diagnoses over the phone when you're half asleep?"

"Of course not."

"Well, neither do I."

A huffy silence followed while I visualized a Napoleon wannabe narrowing his eyes and grinding his teeth.

"Nine A.M. outside the hospital chapel," Quinn capitulated. "If I'm late, wait."

He was a physician. I expected to wait.

***

THE GOOD DOCTOR towered over me by about three inches and exceeded my weight by a mere forty-five pounds. He had a round, doughy face and straight, black hair that scarcely covered his broad pate. I suspect some personality might reveal itself in his smile, but I did not experience that at 9 A.M. outside the hospital chapel, or even at 9:20 when he arrived.

We did not enter the chapel, nor did we sit down anywhere else.

I extended my hand. Quinn didn't notice, so I slipped my arm behind my back and lifted my chin to match his.

"Eight minutes," he said, cheating me by two, so I skipped straight to my first question.

"Did you order a psych eval on Maisie Zumstein?"

"I can't tell you that. If that's the only reason we're here…" He began to turn away.

"Doctor!" I said, folding my arms across my chest and moving to stop him. "Eric Zumstein believes you think he tried to kill his grandmother, an accusation that has impacted a real, live woman's life. I have evidence that may clear up what happened, but first I need some information from you."

Quinn's jaw muscle rolled. "Go on."

"The morning Maisie fell out of bed. Are you sure she was sedated?"

The doctor's cheeks blossomed, and he spun on his heel again. With me close behind he took ten paces and halted in front of a stand-up computer niche.

After some poking and scrolling, Maisie's former physician spoke as if he were questioning the screen. "The order for the sedative is here, but I'm not seeing confirmation it was administered."

"A mistake?" I wondered aloud to mollify the man.

Quinn waffled. "The nurse may have been called away…"

"…and didn't remember to make the note. Or…" *she just plain forgot.*

The doctor's eight-minute deadline had passed, but he showed no sign of leaving. He shoved his fists into his pockets, pursed his lips, and studied the tile floor before he looked up at me.

"Tell me again why this matters."

I shut my eyes and furrowed my brow until I found the right place to begin.

"Cissie Voight and Ronald Voight are friends," I finally began, crossing my fingers in the hope that Quinn wouldn't rush to judgment. "Neighbors who became friends. Okay?"

"Yes."

"So when Eric Zumstein was upset, horrified...actually *furious*, that you doubted his word about Maisie's fall, he shared his outrage with Cissie..." I displayed my palms in that nothing-to-hide gesture, "...on the phone," I clarified, "which her husband, Ronald, probably overheard on a nanny cam. Along with everything else he does to control his wife, Ronald threatened to package your accusation with some outright lies and get Eric arrested. Which, guilty or innocent, would stick to Eric like stink the rest of his life.

"Ronald is abusive, Doctor, and a very accomplished liar. He has a sweet, capable woman believing she's a terrible wife and mother. Also that she's ugly, and stupid, and will never attract another man. He goes ballistic if she doesn't put gas in the car or runs out of mustard. He broke three of her ribs this week, and she's going home to him today, in part because you put doubts in her head about Eric."

The doctor frowned with doubt. "I honestly don't see what the sedative has to do with any of this. Maisie's right elbow was in a cast. She couldn't scratch her nose. How could she possibly pull an IV out of her other arm?"

I couldn't get the paperback out of my purse fast enough. "This was on her bedside tray. Look." I showed him what I'd concluded was a bloodstain. "Maisie could have used the book to push the IV out of her arm—unless she really was sedated. Then your first instinct is probably right; Eric did cause the fall that led to her death. Most likely also the fall that brought her here in the first place."

Hands resting on his hips, Quinn blinked, and stared, and grimaced, as if marveling at the mess I'd presented him.

I hastily outlined the rest—Maisie's flying bricks and clothesline noose, her penchant for mysteries, and the exploding eggs. I especially stressed her hatred for her Lonny, the ex-husband Eric apparently resembled.

"She was on one of her Lonny-rampages that morning, Dr. Quinn. That was why Eric suggested the sedative then went down for coffee."

"Ah, and that's why you asked about a psych eval."

"Correct. Did you do one?"

"I can't answer that," he repeated, but this time his lips twitched.

"I'm late for a meeting. Stay here." He nodded toward the empty chapel. "I'll be back as soon as I can.

I waited on a chair to the side of the sanctuary's door. If any families wanted to make proper use of the chapel, I planned to relocate; but that didn't happen in the forty-five minutes Quinn was gone.

My initial thoughts focused on Eric's fate, which largely depended on whether or not the sedative had been administered. Even if the blood on the edge of the book proved to be Maisie's, no one had witnessed her using it the way I suggested. Subsequently, it had also been handled by far too many hands to be of any use as evidence.

Bottom line: Nothing would ever prove Eric's guilt; but the book, combined with the sedative answer, would confirm his innocence to a satisfactory degree.

As the minutes dragged on, I gave into temptation and web-surfed on my phone.

"Maisie's nurse isn't on duty today," Dr. Quinn called from the doorway. "I'll call her at home." He held the door for me to join him.

"Carol!" he exclaimed after he'd been greeted. "Dr. Quinn here. Sorry to disturb you, but I've got a rather important question…No, no. You're not in any trouble. I just need an honest answer. Let me be quite clear, it's the honest part that matters.

"Do you remember Maisie Zumstein, the elderly woman who…Yes, the single room…Yes, most likely a stroke. She was quite agitated that morning, and I ordered a sedative.

"Now this is the important part, Carol. Do you remember administering the sedative?" Quinn's gaze strayed to me as he listened.

"Oh, oh, right. The emphysema case, of course…No, no, there was nothing noted. I understand. Now about her grandson..." He listened a while longer, thanked the nurse, and hung up. His face was alight, animated, but not entirely happy.

"Just as you thought," he told me. "Carol got called to an emergency. When she got back, Maisie had already fallen."

"What about Eric?"

"She says he arrived shortly after she discovered his grandmother on the floor. He was so shaken he spilled hot coffee on himself. She said he threw the rest away so he wouldn't burn himself again."

Relief rushed to my head and weakened my knees. "So he's innocent."

"It would appear so."

Dr. Quinn rocked back on his heels and smiled, maybe with satisfaction, and perhaps a little at my expense. Who knew? He had a personality after all.

I kissed the guy on the cheek before I realized what I was doing, then ran for the elevator.

I couldn't wait to tell Cissie.

Chapter 46

I FOUND A BENCH tucked into a small, rectangular garden on my way to the hospital's parking garage. The cell coverage was good, and privacy wasn't an issue.

Cissie's phone rang fifteen times before I hung up and called the shelter directly. The woman who answered double checked, but Cissie and her car were gone.

"Yes, home…Yes, *her* home. Where else does she have to go?"

I clenched my fist in front of my teeth and tried to think. A conversation on the Voight's house phone might still be picked up by Ronald's nanny cam, and showing my face anywhere near Cissie might spark another blow-up, this time directed at me. However, my daughter did live next door, and it would be natural for her and Cissie to cross paths as a matter of course.

I reached Chelsea while she was grocery shopping and outlined the problem.

"You suspected Eric!" she railed, as it became obvious I had.

"Can we please skip past that?" I begged. "Right now you need to find a safe way to tell Cissie she can trust the guy."

She said she would get back to me, "when the deed is done."

I waited.

One day.

Two.

I was almost ready to send my daughter next door to borrow a cup of sugar, when she reported that Cissie had come to her.

"I was reading the paper in the backyard with a glass of iced tea, and there she was with Caroline on her hip.

"'I'm so sick of being alone I could scream,' she said. 'You got any more of that tea?'"

"So you told her," I remarked, cutting Chelsea short.

"Yes."

"How did she react?"

"She changed the subject. Turns out that neither of us know how to fry chicken."

"In other words…?"

"She couldn't bear to talk about Eric."

Which made sense. Breaking free from Ronald's grasp would take much more than another man's outstretched hand. Confidence. Courage. A physical place to go, and the means to sustain herself and her child. Cissie had taken one brave step toward escape, and Natalie, and others like Chelsea and I, would eagerly support her again.

First Cissie had to be ready.

***

HIDDEN IN SHADOW, Eric Zumstein leaned against an oak tree at the edge of his opposite neighbor's yard. Diagonally across the street, Cissie's car was once again in the Voight's driveway, blocked in by Ronald's truck.

As twilight began to fall, lights switched on and revealed activity inside. Cheslea and Bobby side by side watching television. The neighborhood spy looking into his refrigerator. And Cissie moving about in the baby's bedroom.

From his vantage point Eric saw her reach for something in the dresser he'd helped put in place, bend down for a new diaper from the bag he knew to be on the floor next to the changing table. He could almost hear her humming as she prepared the baby for bed, a song of his imagination but no less sweet to his ears.

When she was out of sight, he shut his eyes and lowered his head. Soon speaking on the phone would no longer suffice. Cissie knew that, too, and a part of him admired her for breaking off contact. Any choice she made invited serious consequences; he knew that, but this particular decision made his own infinitely more difficult.

He raked his hand through his hair and glanced again at the window. Half a dozen late-season moths circled in the soft light.

"Poor bastards," he whispered into the night air.

***

I'LL FIND OUT if Eric will see me when we get back from our walk," I announced to my audience of one at breakfast Monday morning. Eager as I was to explain everything I'd learned, 7 A.M. was way too early to phone an unemployed bachelor. "In person, of course," I reaffirmed to Fideaux and myself. What I had to say was way too sensitive for the phone, including the answer I found on the Internet to the question no one had asked.

So, naturally, Fideaux rolled in something vile during our walk. Before I allowed him back in the house, I had no choice. I leashed him to the bird-feeder post near the backdoor, changed into work clothes, and hauled, dog shampoo, water buckets, and towels outside.

I was rinsing my uncooperative pet and grumbling when George Donald Elliot arrived. He wore a spotless blue, buttoned-down shirt and crisply pressed, insurance-salesman slacks.

"Hello!" I said, swiping splatter off my cheeks with my t-shirt sleeve. "Didn't hear your car pull up."

"Or the phone either," George remarked. "Hope you don't mind. I thought I might catch you at home."

Delighted to be released, Fideaux frolicked around the yard like a deranged puppy.

"I don't mind," I answered, "if you don't mind me smelling like wet dog."

"No problem," he assured me, but I noticed he inched the folding chair I offered slightly farther away from mine.

"How is Susan holding up?"

"She's leaving for Los Angeles Friday to stay with a friend. I think she has a couple of job interviews lined up." HIs disappointment was painful to see, and I worried that he blamed me.

I mumbled a vague apology, but he waved that away.

"We stopped being close a long time ago," he reflected. "The truth is I never knew how to relate to a daughter, to my daughter, I should say, so I gave her things. Everything but what she wanted."

"Have you talked to her about this?"

The way he pressed his lips together told me it hadn't much helped.

"So you bought her the ticket," I guessed.

"That's what she wanted."

"Not exactly," I disagreed. Airfare to California was not golf clubs or a tuxedo. It was white shirts. "This time you gave her something she needs."

George cocked his head to show me a slow smile. "You're a piece of work, Ginger Struve Barnes. You know that?"

"So I've heard. Now why are you really here?"

He caressed my face with his eyes. Then he told me. My conversation with Eric could wait another half-day.

Chapter 47

THE MORNING RUSH-HOUR traffic already had me edgier than a long-tailed cat in a room full of rocking chairs, so when my cell phone rang I let out a pathetic little, "Eeep." I poked the Bluetooth to answer only because it was Chelsea.

"Eric put his house up for sale!" she exclaimed as the hill ahead of me lit up like a string of red Christmas lights.

"Oh?"

"Yes. Just when I finally got a date for the recording studio."

"What recording studio?"

Behind me Jack bumped his heels against the seat. Ta-thump. Ta-thump.

"I didn't tell you?"

"No." That was probably what Chelsea had wanted to share the day she returned Maisie's paperbacks. At the time, I wouldn't have absorbed the information, let alone cared.

Remembering, Chelsea uttered a thoughtful, "Umm. You're right. I didn't. Anyway, the school grapevine came up with a parent who owns a small recording studio. She agreed to make a demo for Eric cheap, *except now Eric's leaving.*"

"Probably not today," I reasoned, "and I'm on my way to the airport. Mind if I call you later?" A break in the crawl had gotten me up to thirty miles an hour.

"Wait a minute. Where are you going?"

I poked the Bluetooth off and hit the gas. For an hour let her think I was leading an exciting life.

***

MY DAY HAD begun at dawn with Fideaux's needs. It then took me across the Dannehower Bridge to the Cotaldi's rented row home, where I was met by a distraught Susan and gray-faced George. Jack cheered and ran to embrace my legs, whereupon I burst into tears.

The very air pulsed with so much emotional tension that initially we adults exchanged nothing but empathetic eye contact. We dealt with the specifics in short sentences over the lumps in our throats: Where I was to meet Claire, how to identify her, a few details about Jack's potty training success.

Then George scooped up his grandson with a, "Time to go, Champ."

I wiped my nose and hoisted Jack's duffle to my shoulder. Then Susan blinked and gave each of us a last mournful look. When she bent down for the umbrella stroller, her rigid body seemed to break along with her heart.

I had misjudged her, and the proof on her face would remain a vivid memory for many years.

Jack sensed her pain, too. Trying to reach her, he twisted so hard he nearly broke George's grasp and fell onto the street.

At the car, Susan cupped her hand behind the child's head, rubbed his tears with her thumbs, kissed him…and ran back into the house.

Jack's, "Mama, mama, mama," rang in our ears, as George buckled his grandson into the car seat.

"Dada" was conspicuously absent, of course. Flight risk that he was, Mike currently resided in a Minnesota cell awaiting his fate, which, according to my research, might be anything from time served to two years in prison, and/or a fine up to $4,000, not counting legal expenses and transportation costs. Had he used a weapon, abused Jack, or demanded payment for the boy's return, the penalties would have doubled.

At first the sentencing parameters struck me as lenient, especially in contrast to other kidnappings; but then I considered how fraught with complications each case surely was. Mike Swenson/Cotaldi would never be my choice for Father of the Year, and I cannot condone his actions, yet I do sympathize with his feelings toward his son. Fortunately I'm not a Minnesota judge.

Understandably, Philadelphia has a large and active airport.

Crowds of people inch through cattle chutes to drop off luggage then hustle for distant escalators to join lengthy security lines upstairs. I couldn't go far without a boarding pass, so it had been arranged for Claire to meet us near the left-hand escalator on the ground floor of the pier used by her airline.

Instead, she rushed toward us with a three-hundred watt smile and open arms the second we entered through the wide revolving door. The temptation to hug the breath out of Jack must have been overwhelming, but she slowed herself to a stop a few steps away. Wise, since her son's chubby hands had already fisted with fright.

She greeted me with a breathless hello and polite handshake, all while her eyes devoured the sight of her child.

"I never thought…" was all she could manage. Tears glistening, she stooped down to stroller height and touched the boy's hand.

"Hello, Jack," she said at last, using the name that had been agreed upon. "I'm Claire, Mommy Claire. I'm going to give you jelly bread, and red crayons, and all the love you can stand."

"How long do we have?" I inquired out of necessity.

"Half an hour," she answered without glancing up. "It isn't enough, but we can try."

We found a row of empty seats near the window. Angling the stroller so Jack could watch us, I occupied him with a soft cereal bar. Face filled with curiosity, he stared at Claire as if she were magnetized.

"He's smart," I began, something mothers love to hear. "He likes macaroni and cheese, but hates peas…"

Several minutes into our race against the clock I realized I was handing her precious tidbits she would, and should, discover for herself, so I simply spread my hands and stopped talking.

Claire blinked with surprise, but then she got it.

"Yes," she concurred with a fond glance at her son. "We'll be fine."

The silence that fell offered my only chance to ask what I hadn't dared ask the Minneapolis police. Yet the question stuck in my throat.

"What?" Jack's mother encouraged with a lift of her chin.

"Too personal," I deflected. "Never mind."

"After what you've done for me?" She huffed out a laugh. "I think you've earned the right to ask me just about anything."

Confident that she was indeed sincere, I confessed that I couldn't imagine how Mike had eluded the authorities for more than a year. "What with Amber Alerts and all the technology the police have now, how do you suppose he did it?"

Claire's cheeks flushed, and her eyes shut for a moment.

"Mike's smart," she finally began. "Sound familiar? He is also devious, unforgiving, and almost inhumanly patient, especially when it comes to revenge. Our divorce wasn't unique, but it was very, very unpleasant." She waved her head remembering. "I won't bore you with how nasty we were to each other. We just were." She gazed up at the airport's high ceiling.

"After that whole horrible mess was finished, Mike seemed to settle down. God forgive me, I was lulled into believing it was okay for him to have Jack on his assigned weekends."

She exhaled an enormous sigh. Fixed her injured eyes on me.

"About four months later my appendix burst. My sister couldn't get to Minneapolis fast enough, so Mike took Jack. Literally. I didn't even know they were gone until I got released from the hospital three days later."

"He didn't visit you?"

She waved her head. "He was supposed to be watching Jack, right? We spoke briefly on the phone soon after my anesthetic wore off, but by then we weren't really talking. It didn't surprise me that he didn't call again."

"But more than a year…?"

"Like I said. Mike's smart," she repeated, "and vindictive, and patient. I think he'd been planning to kidnap Jack for months."

"The new identity."

"Yep. He even abandoned his car on another street."

The announcement of a flight startled us both. Realizing it was time to go, Claire rose and gathered Jack's things. I followed as far as I could, pushing the stroller and murmuring soothing phrases to the distressed child.

Parting was rough. Claire stiffened as if consumed by worry, and Jack's eyes widened with alarm. His past was being severed from him as surely as if we'd cut off a limb, and by the look on his face he sensed it.

He began to cry.

Watching until they were out of sight, I comforted myself with the fresh knowledge that Claire was no witch. She was an ordinary woman with brown hair and hazel eyes, a couple of extra pounds, and a preference for comfortable clothes. She possessed common sense, compassion, and a prodigious love for her child. What else could I ask of Jack's mother?

Never mind that my insides felt as if they'd been used for a punching bag, I had carried out George's request.

After I dragged myself across the road back to short-term parking and climbed into my car, I called my daughter.

I inquired whether Eric was home, which meant Chelsea had to push a curtain aside to check for his car.

The answer was, "Yes."

Chapter 48

WHEN I CALLED Eric to ask if I might stop by, his response was, "Why? Because misery loves company?"

"No. Because I have some information about Cissie you might like to hear."

He considered for a moment. "A realtor's bringing somebody. I'm supposed to go out."

"We could walk to the park." The weather was ideal for August, seventy-five degrees with just enough breeze to ruffle the trees.

"You're sure I want to hear this?"

"Pretty sure."

When he opened the door, he wore faded gray Bermuda shorts, a t-shirt dotted with holes, and flip-flops that must have accompanied him to college. His hair had been shampooed but not combed, and his beard was at least three days old. Having him leave well before the realtor arrived with a prospective buyer seemed like a pretty good decision.

At the nearby park we settled on a cement bench with wooden slats. Lacy shadows from the honey-locust tree shading us wriggled on the naked ground at our feet. Across the lawn, two boys of about twelve more or less hit a tennis ball back and forth inside a chain-link enclosure. An elderly woman walking a fussy Havanese wandered along the edge of a shallow creek, and an occasional car slipped past on the street behind us. Summer in suburbia, USA.

"Now. What's this about Cissie?" Eric's hangdog expression conveyed sadness, distrust resignation, and impatience in roughly that order.

"I'll get to that, but let me clear up a couple other things first. Equally important," I assured him as if I were swearing an oath.

"Oh?"

"You said Maisie liked to play around with murder methods from the mysteries she read."

"True."

"Which made you think she might be suicidal."

"Yesss…"

I opened my hand. "So you moved in to keep an eye on her, right?"

"I also needed someplace to live."

"But you didn't learn about Maisie's Alzheimers until the psych evaluation, right?"

"How'd you know…?"

Admitting that Dr. Quinn confirmed my suspicion with a silent smile probably wouldn't fly, so I said, "Mystery lovers usually can't leave a new book alone, but Maisie didn't touch the ones I gave her."

"That's it?"

"Not entirely, but I do think she stopped reading a while ago." When her memory began to fail. However, belaboring that wouldn't get me to my point.

"So," I said, drawing Eric's eyes to mine. "How many times did your grandmother try to kill you?"

He jumped as if he'd been zapped.

"Two or three?" I guessed.

Eric rubbed his flaming face. Then he breathed out the word, "Three," with what passed for relief.

"Her first fall…?"

"Not my fault," he insisted. "I went upstairs to get dressed, and Gram lunged at me."

"You ducked out of the way, and…"

"…down she went." He shook off the vision, then laced his hands together behind his knee.

"The poisoned tea might have done it, but the first sip tasted awful. When I spit it out in the sink, what she used was sitting right there."

He showed me a faint scar on his left forearm. "The knife scuffle didn't last long. Took care of that with a band-aid."

"Why didn't you tell anyone?"

"Like who? The police?"

"Maisie had Alzheimers. She could have gotten treatment."

"But I didn't know that, did I? Anyhow, she couldn't afford a nursing facility. Neither could I."

The uncomfortable topics had made him twitchy, so I gestured for us to walk. The woman and her dog were gone, and the intermittent thock of the tennis ball punctuated our conversation nicely.

"You told all this to Cissie?" I inquired as we headed downhill.

"Yes."

"Even what Dr. Quinn implied?"

"Unfortunately, yes." Eric paused to place his fists on his hips and scrutinize the horizon. "Cissie's doubted me ever since."

"You think that's why she stopped speaking to you."

"Of course."

"Well, it isn't."

Eric gawked at me. "What do you mean?"

As we proceeded along the grassy edge of the creek, I reminded him about Ronald threatening to use Dr. Quinn's suspicions to have him arrested. "Contact between you two became much more dangerous that day. For her, and for you."

He stopped to face me. "You're saying Cissie's trying to protect me?"

"She sort of is," I answered, "but that's only part of what's going on."

I inhaled. Exhaled. Finally gave up hunting for the right words and just told him.

"Ronald doesn't just believe he's better than everyone else. He *knows* it. There is no doubt in his mind that he's exceptional, and, therefore, deserves exceptional treatment."

Eric spat out some choice expletives, while I turned uphill.

Continuing, I said, "Nobody else really matters to Ronald, but he knows better than to let that secret out. In public he acts humble, charming, concerned, whatever it takes to convince people he's a nice guy."

"...instead of an angry, controlling sonovabitch."

"Exactly. Cissie gets just enough of the Nice Guy act to lull her into thinking the worst might be over. Sadly, it works. Over and over again!"

"He's really that calculating?"

"He probably doesn't think of it that way, but yes. Apparently abusers invent so many ways to justify themselves it would make your head spin."

Eric's jaw rolled. "Why doesn't Cissie leave?"

"I asked that, too. Remember, Ronald's had years to bully her into a corner, but he probably caught on that she would be vulnerable to that early on. Did she tell you her family thought she was marrying up?"

"No."

"Well, they did, and it didn't sound like a joke to me."

Now Eric was blinking mad. "But Cissie's great. She's bright. Funny. Sweet. You've seen her with Caroline. She's a wonderful mother!"

"Granted," I said. "But she doesn't hear that from her husband, who, by the way, had no difficulty cutting her off her from her family. He also bad-mouthed all her friends until she quit having any. I got that message without him saying a word."

Eric's distress was headed toward the red zone, so I spared him the final eye-opener I'd gleaned from Natalie's reading material.

Ronald's "Blonde Bitch" lies were more than an excuse for his cheating. If Cissie ever summoned the nerve to turn him in, his friends and coworkers would be armed with years of stories about what a terrible wife and mother she was. Hearing those same complaints herself pretty much every day, Cissie knew precisely what Ronald would tell the judge at a custody hearing. I suspected the prospect of losing Caroline frightened her even more than Ronald's fists.

I rested a hand on Eric's arm. "Let's get to the good news."

"What?" he challenged, as if there were no good news to be had in the world.

"Dr. Quinn knows you're innocent."

"You're kidding. How?"

I filled him in on how the nurse got delayed giving Maisie the sedative, and my theory about the blood on the edge of the paperback. I also told him I'd learned something interesting about Alzheimers' medications on the Internet.

"Did you know they can increase the risk of a stroke?"

"Do you think that was what happened?"

I lifted one shoulder as if I didn't know. "You said Maisie was revved up about Lonny even worse than usual. What do you think?"

Eric ran his hand through his tangled hair. "I don't know what to think."

We ambled back toward his house in silence.

"I should have done more for Gram," he lamented when we reached his sidewalk.

"You did as much as anyone could."

Eric rolled his eyes.

"You've got a lot to process," I said. "You'll get there."

"Cissie still won't speak to me."

"But now you know why."

A tight-lipped sneer.

"I know. Easy for me to say," I admitted, "but think of it this way. If you leave, you can't be her soft landing. If you stay, maybe you can."

Chapter 49

SEPTEMBER 1 offered puffy white clouds and heat nearing ninety. I filled Fideaux's kiddie pool, purchased on a whim on closeout, and donned cut-off shorts and my Alaska-or-Bust t-shirt. I had no expectations of the day except for breakfast, lunch, and dinner. I was slightly wrong.

A florist's truck chugged to a stop at my mailbox like an angry coffeepot exhaling its last breath.

"Hey, ho, Ms. Barnes," said the young deliveryman. I thought maybe he was happy his summer job was nearly over so he could go back to school.

"That's me," I agreed.

He handed me an arrangement wrapped in green tissue.

I took it inside to the kitchen counter. It wasn't overly large, nor overly small. It consisted primarily of red carnations enhanced by sprigs of baby's breath and fern. Stuck into the clear plastic harp they use to hold cards was a rectangle of white that read, "Thank you!"

The envelope that should have contained the sender's name proved to be empty.

Ordinarily I'd have phoned the florist to ask for more information, but the truck was long gone, and I hadn't noted the company name. Saying thank-you for a thank-you gift was ridiculous anyhow. The exchange could go back and forth for months.

Speculating was fun, though.

George?

Certainly not Mike Cotaldi or Ronald. Not The Hunter either. We circled wide whenever we encountered each other.

Susan was already in California interviewing for jobs.

Claire? Unlikely. She was too over-the-moon with Jack to give me the slightest thought.

Eric? Chelsea had called three days after my last conversation with her next door neighbor.

"Guess what," she demanded.

"You're pregnant."

"Never say that to me again."

"Okay."

"Promise?"

"Absolutely."

"Eric took down the For Sale sign. Bent it in half and stuffed it into the trash. You know what that means, don't you?"

Whaddya know? He was sticking around. Good man!

Which Chelsea knew well before I did, so I ribbed her and said, "He can make his recording date after all."

"You're having one of those days, aren't you?"

"Yeah, I guess I am."

I haven't yet learned who sent the carnations, nor do I care to find out.

What's life without a little mystery?

\#

Dear Reader—If you enjoyed FOR BETTER OR WORSE, here are two reasons to post a **brief review** at the online bookseller of your choice (while it's still fresh in your mind). <u>Fellow readers will greatly appreciate your advice</u>, *and* it's the easiest way to make an independent author very, very happy.

Interested in being the first to hear about a special bargain, a new release, a tempting contest, or maybe just some good news? Please join my **email list** (free book involved). Link on my website: donnahustonmurray.com.

Many thanks!

Donna

PS: **Book Club** discussion questions on request. If you'd like me to join your meeting via Skype or Facetime, please e-mail me from my website, and we'll figure it out.

Acknowledgements

I am indebted to many people for their help with this very personal project: Kristy Carnahan; Lundy Bancroft (as referenced by Gin) for his excellent book, WHY DOES HE DO THAT, and Meg Kennedy Dugan and Roger R. Hock for their book, IT'S MY LIFE NOW. Thanks, too, to my team of experts, Robynne Graffam, Hench Murray, Nancy Winter, proofreader Paula Grundy, Sonja Haggert, April Weston, Elissa Strati, Alan Meeds, and Officer Joseph Butler. Cover designer, Alexandra Albornoz Sarmiento did a splendid job with Eduard Moldoveanu's beautiful photograph of Philadelphia's Boathouse Row, and Michael Redmond deserves credit for taking a picture of me.

Most of all I am grateful for my amazing mother, Ruth M. Ballard, for being an exemplary role model of grace under pressure, and for so much more.

Donna

In real life Donna assumes she can fix anything until proven wrong, calls trash-picking recycling, and, although she probably should know better, adores Irish setters.

Donna and husband, Hench, live in the greater Philadelphia, PA, area. They have two adult children.

More @ http://www.donnahustonmurray.com

GET HELP

If you are in danger call 911

FOR ANONYMOUS, CONFIDENTIAL HELP,
24/7, PLEASE CALL:

NATIONAL
DOMESTIC VIOLENCE
HOTLINE

1-800-799-SAFE (7233)
1-800-787-3224 (TTY)

CPSIA information can be obtained
at www.ICGtesting.com
Printed in the USA
BVOW03s2132281217
503944BV00001B/7/P